Top Hands

Stu Campbell

ISBN: 978-0-9988499-6-6

6   5   4   3   2   1

Edited by Mira Perrizo
Cover and text design by D.K. Luraas
Cover painting by R. Loren Schmidt
Author photo by Elizabeth Dobbs

Printed in the United States of America

Contents

ONE
Putting a Crew Together

They were all good hands, the kind of cowboys—or buckaroos—that could work on any
cow outfit. They didn't all arrive together, they
just sorta drifted in, one at a time.

The first to come was Will Claxton. He was
almost six feet tall, and tanned with the look of
someone who had spent all his life outdoors.
He'd been in some trouble with the law in the
past, but that was all behind him now. He got a
full reprieve from the judge that sentenced him
in exchange for helping put the crooks behind
bars. He wasn't proud of the time he'd spent in
jail and didn't talk about it.

Will had hired on in January to help with the
calving, even though it was early. There wasn't
much riding to do, just go through the cattle each
day looking for something that might be wrong.
The cows weren't supposed to start calving until

the middle of February. The most serious condition he came across in January was a prolapsed cow. He brought her into the corrals, put her in a squeeze chute, and sewed her up using baling twine knowing that when she calved it would rip loose. He marked her with some paint similar to what the Forest Service used so he could keep an eye on her in the future.

The owner of the ranch had pointed out a string of four horses that Will could consider his while he worked for the outfit. "There ain't no buck in any of 'em," said the ranch owner. "They're all solid, honest as the day is long horses. The roan tends to get a little anxious comin' home. Seems like he kinda wants to hurry home an' get the day over quicker. But he's a good one."

Will looked over each horse carefully, memorizing what their features were.

The ranch already had a cook, a grizzled old timer. He was a pretty good cook and quite proud of his sourdough bread and biscuits. He talked a lot, mostly to the items he was cooking up. It almost seemed like he was coaxing his cooking along. He was known simply as "Cookie."

A few days later another hand was hired on.

His name was Kent. The owner of the ranch, Tom Zimmerman, hired Kent, saying, "We're not due to start calvin' till the middle of February. I've got one man hired so far, but we'll need a few more. You can help Will, although there ain't much to do yet. That'll change before long. Come out to the corral an' I'll point out your string of horses an' introduce you to Will."

They walked out to the corrals. Will was just coming in from riding through the cattle. Tom pointed out Kent's horses to him as they waited for Will to arrive.

Will rode directly to the barn and started unsaddling his horse. Tom and Kent walked over to him.

"Will," said Tom, "this is Kent. I just hired him to help you out."

After Will put his saddle on its rack, he shook hands with Kent. "Pleased to meet you," he said. "Don't need much help right now."

"Same here," replied Kent.

Tom said, "There ain't much goin' on now, but that'll change before long."

Both men quietly sized each other up. They were about the same size and build. There didn't appear to be any tension between the men as they looked each other over.

"I'll show you where the bunkhouse is," Tom told Kent. "Get your bedroll."

Kent got his bedroll from his car and followed Tom to the bunkhouse. "You can take any bunk you want," said Tom. "Will's already got that one. Supper should be ready 'bout six-thirty in the big house."

Soon Will came to the bunkhouse and the two men visited quietly about the different ranches they'd worked on. The talk was soft and not very animated.

At supper, the talk was more animated and louder, with Cookie leading the conversation. He had an opinion on anything and considered himself an expert on everything.

After supper, as Will and Kent walked to the bunkhouse, Kent remarked, "That Cookie can sure talk. I don't think he paused long enough to see if anyone was even listening!"

"Yep," replied Will.

"I'll bet he can carry on a conversation with himself an' not even repeat himself," said Kent.

"Yep," answered Will.

"I wonder," said Kent, "when he gets into an argument with himself, how does he tell who won?"

Will grunted in a sort of laugh. "I don't know how he determines the winner. With himself, it has to be him!"

Kent laughed. "I guess you're right! I wonder how it would be, to be right all the time!"

The next morning, Will, Kent and Tom saddled their horses and rode out through the cattle. Will and Tom paid close attention to how Kent saddled his horse and got on him. Watching Kent, they both knew he'd had plenty of horse experience in the past.

Tom and Kent rode out together and Will followed. Tom pointed out various aspects of the ranch to Kent much the same way he'd done with Will on Will's first day.

Will pointed out the cow that had prolapsed to Tom. "Keep a pretty close eye on her," said Tom. "She may need some extra help when she calves."

A few days later another hand got hired on. He was known as Slim. He never gave his real name.

Tom pointed out a string of horses to Slim and gave him some information on each one of them. Slim listened quietly and looked over each horse and memorized them.

At supper that night, the men talked quietly.

Cookie led the conversation, asking a lot of questions of Slim. Slim answered the questions and appeared to be polite to the questioning.

After supper on the way to the bunkhouse, Slim said, "That cook sure asks a lot of questions. Does he remember all the answers?"

"I don't know," replied Will, laughing. "If he does he'll become a storehouse of information."

The next day as everyone saddled their horses, they kept an eye on Slim, quietly watching as he saddled his horse. Each man was making his own determination as to what kind of hand Slim was.

Slim saddled his horse, untracked him, cheeked him and stepped on. Tom, Will and Kent watched as Slim got on. Each man was satisfied that Slim knew what he was doing.

Tom got on his horse and rode over to Slim. "You don't have to cheek any of these horses. They're all broke good."

"Just force of habit," replied Slim. "I cheek everything until I know 'em."

Tom just nodded, knowingly.

All three men rode out with Tom, giving Slim some general information regarding the lay of the land as they rode. Will and Kent followed, not saying anything.

A few days later two more hands showed up. They arrived the same day, about ten minutes apart. One was Pete Peterson and the other was George Knowles. Pete was about the same age as Will, Kent and Slim, but George was considerably older, close to sixty, if not older.

"You boys travelin' together?" asked Tom.

"Nope," replied Pete. "I come alone," he said, handing Tom the papers that the employment agency had given him.

"The employment agency sent me out, too," said George, giving Tom the papers he'd got at the employment agency. "They told me you were lookin' for help."

"This will give me five hands, six countin' myself," said Tom. "That's all I need. We'll calve out my cows, brand the calves, haul some salt an' scatter some bulls. I've got about six hundred yearlings that need to be gathered an' shipped, then we'll be done. The job will last till about the middle of July. You interested?"

"Yep," answered Pete.

"Any chance you got anything past that?" asked George.

"Not really," replied Tom. "There's still some salt to be hauled, but I can pretty well handle that."

"I was actually lookin' for somethin' that lasted longer," said George.

"I'm ready to start work right now," said Pete.

"Good," said Tom. "What about you?"

"I guess so," replied George.

Tom cast a questioning eye at George, then said, "I'll introduce you to the other hands an' we'll get you a string of horses an' go out in the mornin'. Put your bedrolls in the bunkhouse over there."

Tom pointed to the bunkhouse. "Supper will be ready about six-thirty," he added. "You boys can set up housekeepin' till then. The other hands will be in shortly."

Pete and George parked their cars in front of the bunkhouse, took their bedrolls and extra clothes inside, and then waited for the other hands to show up.

"I'll sure be glad when them other hands show up. It'll be 'bout suppertime an' I ain't et since mornin'," said George.

"Yeah, it's been a spell since I had somethin' myself," replied Pete. "Think I'll stretch out on a bunk an' catch some shut-eye."

At supper that night the men started talking about where they'd worked previously. When Pete mentioned he'd worked for Charlie over at the Flyin' N, everyone took notice. Apparently everyone had heard of it.

"I'd like to hire on a good outfit like the Flyin' N," said Slim. "I hear them hands don't leave there. Good job security."

Finally, Will asked, "How come you left there? I heard that's a good outfit an' they don't need any help. If a feller gets hired on there, he generally stays."

"That is a good outfit," said Pete. "I only hired on to halter break some mustang colts for 'em. The feller that does the halter breakin' broke his leg an' couldn't do it."

"What's that outfit doin' with mustang colts?" asked Tom. "They got high dollar, registered horses."

"Charlie took 'em on as a favor for the BLM man," said Pete. "Do you know Charlie?"

"No," answered Tom. "But I've seen some of the horses he's trained. He does a good job."

"How come you left?" asked George. Apparently he hadn't been listening.

"I got the colts gentled down an' halter broke," replied Pete. "Charlie already had a full crew. There wasn't anything else to do. He did say to keep in touch."

Wanting to change the subject from himself

to someone else, he asked, "Where you from, George?"

"Arizona mostly," answered George. "But I been just about everywhere. I worked most of the big outfits in Arizona. It gets mighty hot down there in the summer if you can't get on an outfit that has some mountain range."

"You'll cool off plenty up here this winter," said Tom. "Winter ain't over yet an' we can still get some pretty cold days. There's still snow in the forecast."

"I don't much care for the snow or the cold," said George.

"Then how come you're up here?" asked Slim.

"I heard the chances of gettin' on up here were better durin' the calvin' season an' the chances of stayin' on till fall were better," replied George.

"That's generally true," said Tom. "But you need a bigger outfit than this one. I only got about fifteen hundred head of cows. But they're scattered over a lot of ground. I could really put more cows on the range, but I always have plenty of feed left in the fall. Don't need much help after brandin'. I can handle the packin' salt. But the six of us will be plenty busy till summer."

The talk continued about where the hands had worked in the past. Then Tom said, "We'll finish calvin' these cows out. As the cows calve, we'll turn 'em out on the desert. Then we'll go out an' stay in a cow camp while we brand. We'll be out in camp just about two months, brandin' calves, scatterin' bulls an' haulin' salt. We do have about six hundred head of yearlin's to gather an' ship. We should be done around the fourth of July."

"Nothin' after that?" asked George.

"I'm afraid not," replied Tom. "I can handle everything after that by myself. If you're lookin' for more work, you might check with my brother. He's in charge of the farmin'. He might need some extra help."

"I ain't interested in farmin'," said George.

"You better tell me now if you're goin' to stay on till we're done brandin'," said Tom.

"I'm here, I might just as well," answered George.

"When the cows calve," said Tom, "we'll turn 'em out on the desert. There's still plenty of feed out there. It's dry feed, but it's good feed. Then we'll gather, brand the calves an' take 'em to the mountain every couple of days. When the rains come, the feed will get better."

All the other hands—Will, Pete, Kent and Slim—listened as Tom told George the plan. George seemed to be a cantankerous sort of individual and Will made a whispered comment to Pete, "He seems to be a sort of ornery kind of individual."

"I think he'll be kinda hard to deal with," said Pete. "I hope Tom knows what he's doin'."

"He's been around, he should," said Kent.

"We'll make a camp out there when the weather warms up," said Tom. "After school's out, I'll have a high school kid come out an' he'll be our jingle boy. He's jingled the horses for me in the past and, for his age, he's a pretty good hand. There's a good pasture we can keep the horses in durin' the day until the kid comes."

The following day everyone rode out through the cattle. The cattle weren't scattered, but they were in a fairly large pasture and it took one man a long time to ride through it. Tom took everyone all around the pasture, pointing out where they needed to be sure and check for cows that might be calving.

George asked, "Do you have a set of corrals where we can bring cows into that might be needin' some help?"

"Yep," replied Tom. "It's in the middle of

this pasture. I'll show you where it is when we're done."

They continued riding the pasture. They had to cross a few streams. "These creeks is where the cattle water out here. The larger streams run year round, but the smaller streams tend to freeze up. You might have to bring an axe out to open 'em up so the cattle can drink."

They continued riding the pasture and when they crossed the last stream, Tom said, "The corrals are just over that rise. Anybody want a cup of coffee? Are you cold?"

George was the first to answer with a hardy, "You bet! It's colder than a mother-in-law's kiss out here."

His comment brought a laugh from the other hands.

"Well, there's a coffee pot at the corrals an' a can of coffee by the gatepost. There's also some cups in a gunny sack tied on a post. There's firewood close by. George, you get the pot an' fill it at the stream. Make sure you rinse it out good, there's probably goin' to be some rust in it. An' get the water upstream from where the cattle have been waterin'. I don't want my coffee tainted with the taste of cow! The rest of us will gather up some fire wood an' start a fire."

When they got to the corrals, George found the coffee pot and went to fill it.

"Make sure you rinse it out good!" yelled Tom as George rode off.

George raised the pot over his head in acknowledgment and continued riding. Everyone else got off their horses, hobbled them and gathered up some dry brush and started a fire. Tom got the coffee from where he'd cached it the last time he used it.

A good fire was going when George got back and the hands were warming themselves. George handed the pot to Tom.

"It's only half full!" exclaimed Tom. "Why didn't you fill it all the way?"

"It was full when I left. I guess I spilled some comin' back here. I almost fell off gettin' the water I got!" answered George. "There's enough for everybody to get a cup."

"Did you rinse it out good?" asked Tom.

"As good as I could," replied George.

"What's these brown an' black things floatin' on top?" asked Tom.

"Brown things? What brown an' black things?" questioned George.

"These," said Tom as he poured out the water.

As the water flowed out, everyone saw pieces of rust and some dead bugs come out with the water.

"Looks like rust an' some dead bugs," said Tom.

George got off his horse, hobbled him and went to the fire to warm himself up. He stayed quiet.

Slim went to his horse, took the hobbles off him, rode over to Tom and said, "Give me the pot. I'll rinse it out good an' bring it back full."

When Slim left, Kent said, "That Slim don't say much, but when he does say somethin', it counts."

"You're right," said Pete.

Soon Slim returned with the coffee pot and handed it to Tom.

"Look here," said Tom. "It's full!"

"An' there ain't no floaters in it," said Slim as he cast a disgusted look at George and hobbled his horse.

Tom got a cup from the gunny sack, filled it with snow and set it on the fire. When the snow melted, he swished the water around in the cup and rinsed it out.

"We've got a good fire goin'," said Tom as he poured some water into the cup he'd cleaned and dumped some coffee into the pot. "We'll have her boilin' before too long."

Everyone stayed quiet while the water came to a boil, but they were all thinking the same thing: just what kind of a hand was this guy George and what kind of person was he?

"Takes a little while for the water to boil, cold as it is," said Will.

"I'd have brought hot water if I'd have known where to find it," said Slim.

Everyone laughed at Slim's comment, everyone except George. He was apart from the others but still close enough to the fire to get warm.

Soon the coffee pot was boiling and Tom took the cup of water he'd saved and poured it into the pot. "That'll settle the grounds," he said as he took the pot off the fire.

"Anybody ready for a cup of coffee?" he asked. "I'm sorry I ain't got no cream an' sugar, you'll have to take it black. But it's ready. Get your cups from that gunny sack."

Everyone went to the gunny sack. Pete held it open for everybody to get a cup. George was the last to get his cup.

"You might want to put some clean snow in your cup, melt it on the fire an' rinse it out before you get the coffee, just like Tom did," said

Pete when everyone had a cup. "That's what I'm gonna do."

"Good idea," said Kent as he filled his cup with snow.

George went straight to Tom to get his coffee.

Tom asked, "You ain't goin' to rinse out your cup?"

"Nope," said George. "I bet that coffee's strong enough to kill anything! I seen how much grounds you put in the pot."

The other hands lined out behind George and waited their turn for coffee. When everyone had a full cup, Tom filled his own cup and set the pot down, close enough to the fire to keep it hot.

As they drank the coffee and enjoyed the heat from the fire, Tom said, "Tomorrow we'll split up into pairs. With three pairs we should be able to ride through all the cattle in half the time. We'll have some pretty easy days for a spell. George will ride with me an' you guys can figure out who you want to ride with."

"Makes no difference to me," said Kent.

"Me neither," said Will.

The other hands said they didn't care, but in each one's mind was the thought, *I don't particularly want to ride with George.*

"Anyone want more coffee?" asked Tom.

George stepped forward and stuck out his empty cup. "Sure," he said.

"How's 'bout you, Will? There's plenty," said Tom.

"Half a cup," replied Will. He held his cup out.

"An' you Pete?"

"Nope," replied Pete. "I think what I've had will rot my innards!"

Everyone laughed.

"You Kent? An' you Slim?" asked Tom.

"Half a cup," answered Kent, holding out his cup.

"Me too," said Slim, extending his cup.

"Better get what you can," said Tom as he poured himself a half a cup. "It'll be a cold ride home."

TWO
Some Animosity Builds

When everyone finished their coffee, they followed Tom's example, filling the empty cups with snow, setting them on the fire and when the snow melted, rinsing out the cups. They put them in the gunny sack and Tom tied it to the post. He'd already put the lid on the coffee can and set it by the post.

Everyone caught up their horses, took off the hobbles, mounted and started for the ranch. It was a cold ride back to the ranch. A wind had come up and they were riding right into it. There wasn't much said on the way home.

When they got to the ranch, they grained their horses, everyone except George, and unsaddled them.

"Aren't you goin' to grain your horse?" Tom asked George.

"I don't think he needs it," answered George.

"Well, he does," said Tom, handing George a nosebag with grain in it. "Here, give him this, he's carried you around all day. He's earned a little reward."

When the horses had finished their grain, they turned them loose in the corral.

"I'll check with the cook an' see when supper's ready. Cookie will holler at you when it's ready."

Tom went to the house. After he'd left, George said to Will, "He's a tough ol' bird, ain't he." It was more of a statement than a question.

"I guess so," replied Will. "But I got a pretty good idea he knows what he's doin'."

Supper was quiet that night for everybody except the cook and George. Everyone seemed to have acquired a certain dislike for George, but didn't necessarily want to show it.

"You boys are might quiet tonight," said George when the cook paused to catch his breath. They'd been talking about current affairs and Cookie had been relating the news of the day as he'd seen it on television.

Nobody said anything and George gave everyone a queer look. Finally Will said, "Hungry. That coffee was good today, but it didn't go far enough."

"Yeah," said George. "It was mighty good. I think tomorrow I'll take some cream an' sugar out there."

"Yeah," said Slim sarcastically, "better take a spoon to stir it, too!"

Slim's comment brought some laughter from the other hands.

"Better bring a tablecloth, too!" said Pete.

"A tablecloth! What for?" questioned George.

"Well, you can set it on that rock an' have yourself a little tea, er, coffee party," replied Pete.

"That's a good idea, but I think you guys are funnin' me!" said George.

"Suit yourself," said Pete.

Tom interrupted the conversation when he said, "You guys figure out who you want to ride with tomorrow. George will ride with me. We'll split up at the gate an' meet back at the corrals. Splittin' up like that, we should get done in half the time."

"Don't make no difference to me who I ride with," said Kent. "Anybody will do."

"Same here," said Will.

"Okay," said Tom. "You two go together an' Pete an' Slim can go together. It'll be a pretty easy day an' we should get done fairly early. The long days will come when we start calvin'. Better hit the sack, we'll be up early."

"Don't forget the tablecloth an' the sugar an' cream," said Pete.

"An' be sure to bring along some biscuits!" added Kent. "Cake would be better!"

They left the kitchen laughing.

The next morning, they were all up early. George needed some shaking before he came awake, but was only a few minutes late for breakfast. They saddled fresh horses and headed out.

When they got to the pasture where the cattle were, Tom said, "Will, you an' Kent go to the right an' Pete, you an' Slim go to the left. George an' I will cover the middle. We'll meet at the corrals."

"Okay," they all agreed.

As they left, Kent yelled, "You got the cake, George? An' the cream an' sugar?"

They parted and went their separate ways, laughing. Far enough away from the others, Kent said to Will, "That George seems to be a character, don't he?"

"It appears that way," said Will. "I don't think Tom was too happy when he brought the coffee pot back only half full an' with some floaters in it."

"No, I don't think he was either. I'm developin' a small dislike for him."

"I don't much care for him either," replied Will. "I sure wouldn't want to partner up with him."

"Did you hear the way he snored last night?" questioned Kent. "Woke me up an' I had a hard time gettin' back to sleep."

"I heard him all right. Sounded just like a locomotive."

"Yeah."

The men rode their area, carefully checking all the cattle they saw, then they headed toward the corrals. When they arrived, Tom and George were already there. They had a fire going and there was coffee brewing on it.

"Coffee's ready," said Tom. "I got the water," added Tom, as if to reassure the men that the water was clean.

George was warming himself by the fire, holding his metal coffee cup in gloved hands.

Will and Kent got off their horses, unbridled and hobbled them and turned them loose. They got cups from the gunny sack, filled them with snow and let the snow melt with the cups on the fire. They rinsed the cups and filled them with coffee.

"Where's the cream an' sugar? An' the table-cloth?" asked Kent.

"Ah, quit ridin' me," said George. "I didn't bring any."

"I'm disappointed," said Kent. "I was lookin' forward to it, maybe even livin' like civilized folks."

"You want cream an' sugar, you bring it!" retorted George.

George's tone of voice brought a stern look from Tom. He'd already decided that maybe George wasn't going to fit in well with the others. The others all seemed to get along, but George didn't seem to fit in well. Tom thought he might have a problem, but decided not to do anything about it until it became a real problem. Tom also decided he'd have to keep an eye on George.

Slim and Pete showed up while George was having his second cup of coffee.

"There's some ol' heifers really springin' out there," said Pete. "When are they supposed to start calvin'?"

"They're supposed to start around the middle of February," Tom answered. "It ain't that far away."

"I'll bet they start before that," said Slim.

"Well, we'll be ready for 'em," said Tom.

"We've got a full crew now. We might have to start earlier in the mornin'."

"We ought to bring out more coffee tomorrow," said George. "This can is about done for."

"You can get another can from the cook in the mornin'," said Tom.

"An' don't forget the cream an' sugar, like you did today," said Pete.

George gave Pete a dirty look, but didn't say anything.

When Slim and Pete had gotten their coffee, Tom took Pete off to the side and said in a lowered voice, "You need to lay off George, Pete. He's kind of a sensitive ol' buzzard."

"I'm just funnin' with him," said Pete.

"I know," replied Tom, "but he ain't takin' it well. I'm really not sure what kind of a hand he is, but I need everybody we got an' you're funnin' with him might run him off."

"We might be better off without him," replied Pete. "His snorin' will keep everyone awake all night when we move into the tent."

"That might be," answered Tom. "But we'll see. I had him ride with me today because I detected some animosity between him an' the others."

Pete asked, "How did you two get along?"

"Good enough, I suppose. But he talked all mornin'. He don't shut up. I had to send him off alone just to get some relief."

When Pete and Slim finished their coffee, everyone caught their horses and rode back to the ranch.

"Breakfast will be earlier in the mornin'," said Tom while they were unsaddling their horses. "I'll tell the cook."

The next day, all the hands rode through the cattle, but nobody saw anything that needed to be brought in. They met at the corrals, had their coffee and rode back to the ranch.

George had brought another can of coffee, but didn't bring any cream and sugar.

They all rode out the following day on fresh horses. It had snowed the night before and there was about three inches of fresh snow on the ground. They split up again, paired up the same as they had been for the previous couple of days, and they rode the same part of the big pasture they'd rode before.

Tom and George came across a young heifer that was calving. Everything appeared to be normal and Tom told George, "You stay here an' make sure everything is okay. If she has any problems, bring her to the corrals. I'll meet you there after I ride through the rest of the cattle."

Tom rode off and finding no other situations, rode to the corrals. He was surprised to not find George there. He thought George would have already arrived, had a fire going and the coffee on.

I better go out an' look for him, Tom thought.

He rode back to where he'd left George and found a newborn calf, but there wasn't any sign of George or the heifer. After making sure the calf was okay, Tom rode out to look for George.

After a few minutes and over a small rise in the ground, he saw George, chasing a cow full speed in the distance.

Tom took a direct route to where he thought he'd intercept George and met him and the heifer. He stopped George.

"What's goin' on?" he asked.

"That ol' heifer dropped her calf, turned around, took one look at him an' took off runnin' as fast as she could. I been tryin' to get her back to the calf."

"That ain't an ol' heifer," replied Tom. "That's a first calf heifer. Quite often, they'll drop a calf, run around the area, an' then come back to the calf. I suppose it's a trying experience for them, bein' first calvers. Just leave her alone an' see if she goes back to the calf."

They rode back to the corrals. On the way, George asked, "You already been here an got the coffee on?"

"I been here, but ain't started any coffee." replied Tom. "I thought you might need some help an' went lookin' for you. Besides that, this ain't no picnic we're havin' out here."

They got to the corrals before anyone else. Tom got the coffee pot and went to the creek for water. George hobbled his horse and started a fire. Tom returned with a pot of water, handed it to George, hobbled his horse and went to the fire to warm up.

"I started the coffee," said George.

"Did you pour out a cup to use to settle the grounds?"

"No," answered George. "I forgot."

Tom gave George a disgusted look and filled a cup with fresh snow and put it on the fire to melt.

The coffee was boiling when Will and Kent rode in.

"There's some new calves out there this mornin'," said Will. "Only three, but they're okay. There's a lot more springers. We'll be plenty busy here shortly."

Tom said, "Slim, you grab a cup of coffee, warm up a little, then come with me."

"I'm ready right now," replied Slim.

"Good!"

Tom got his horse, took the hobbles off him and got on.

As they rode out, Tom said to Slim, "George an' I came across a heifer calvin'. I left George to keep an eye on her an' when I got back, both George an' the heifer were gone. The calf was okay so I started lookin' for George. Found him an' the heifer runnin' like the devil. George said the heifer had took off after she'd dropped the calf, an' he was tryin' to bring her back. I just want to check an' see if she made it back."

"Don't he know that them first calvers will run off after droppin' a calf then they'll usually return?" asked Slim.

"Apparently not," replied Tom.

They got to where the calf was and found the heifer licking off the calf. The calf was trying to stand and quite wobbly.

The men watched from a distance for a few minutes, then Tom said, "Everything seems to be all right here. Let's go back."

On the way back, Tom asked Slim, "What do you make of George?"

"I don't rightly know," answered Slim. "He talks a lot an' his snorin' is pretty loud."

Slim was being as noncommittal as possible, knowing he had to work with everyone at least until spring and they were done branding.

"Now, you tell me the truth."

"That's as much as I know," replied Slim. "I'd bet though that he's the kind that wants to get paid for standin' around drinkin' coffee rather than doin' what he's actually bein' paid to do."

Tom didn't say anything, but let Slim's words sink in.

Presently, Tom asked, "What do you think of the other hands?"

"They all appear to be pretty good hands, but I ain't rode with any of them except Pete. I think he knows what he's doin'."

Tom managed to ride alone with the other hands and asked each one what they thought of George. For the most part, they were noncommittal, not wanting to degrade one of their co-workers in front of the boss. Among themselves, they were more open, speaking quite frankly. George was not held in high esteem among them.

When they got to the corrals, they hobbled their horses and went to the fire.

"Get a cup," said Tom.

They drank their coffee, George having finished his second cup, and rode back to the ranch.

Having taken care of their horses, they all went to the bunkhouse, except George. He went to the kitchen to talk to Cookie.

"Them boys don't say much," he said to the cook as he went into the kitchen. "Got any coffee?"

"There's some on the stove," answered the cook.

George poured himself a cup and sat down at the table. The two men talked, each one trying to outdo the other one.

Presently, the cook asked George, "Will you go to the bunkhouse an' tell the boys that supper's ready?"

George went to the door and yelled, "Supper's ready!"

"No," said the cook. "Go to the bunkhouse an' tell them."

George gave the cook a surprised look and went to the bunkhouse. The men had been talking, but when George arrived, it suddenly became quiet.

George stuck his head in the doorway, said, "Supper's ready," and returned to the kitchen. The other men followed.

Supper was quiet, other than George and Cookie conversing. What they were talking about didn't much matter to the others.

For the next few weeks, the routine was pretty much the same, riding through the cows looking for anything that might need help calving. There were a few cows that needed help—the calves were being born backward. The men did what they could for them, saving a few and losing a few.

George became the self-appointed coffee maker, quite often leaving Tom alone to pull a calf while he made coffee. Tom didn't say anything, there wasn't much George could do.

Tom was becoming a little upset with George and was disappointed in him and his work. However, he needed a crew of five plus himself to do the branding—two men to rope calves, two men to keep the cattle in a semblance of a herd and two men on the ground to brand, vaccinate, earmark and castrate.

***

Before long, most of the cows had calved and Tom told the crew, "Tomorrow, we'll turn the cows out. We're 'bout done calvin' an' we'll get ready to go out on the wagon an' brand the calves. I'll have to take Cookie to town an' get supplies the next day. If any of you want to go to town, when I go will be the time. But you'll need to be here early the following day so we can go set up camp. We'll need to set up two tents, one for the cook an' one for us."

"I don't need anything in town," said Will.

The general consensus among the others was the same as Will had expressed, except for George.

"There is some things I need from town," he said.

"You can ride into town with Cookie an' me," volunteered Tom.

"I'll take my car," said George. "It'll be kinda crowded with the three of us in the truck."

They turned the cows and calves out the following day. The day after, Tom and the cook went to town and George followed them in his car.

When Tom returned to the ranch, he noticed that George's car was not back yet. He went to the bunkhouse and asked, "Anybody seen George?"

"Nope," said Pete.

"He ain't got back yet," said Kent.

"I don't know where he went when he got to town," said Tom. "He'd better make it back, or we'll be a man short."

The four hands just shrugged their shoulders, secretly hoping George wouldn't return.

The cook had left the supplies in the back of the truck, knowing that they'd be ready to go to camp. He loaded the two tents in the truck and fixed supper.

At supper that night, the cook said, "You boys throw your bedrolls in the back of the truck in the mornin' or you'll have to sleep without 'em in camp."

Tom said, "Cookie knows where to set up camp. He'll go out in the mornin' an' start. We'll follow horseback an' bring the horses. George ain't showed up yet. I hope he gets here. Worthless as he is, we'll need him."

After supper, the men went to the bunkhouse and Tom went into his office and made a phone call.

When the men went to bed, George still hadn't showed up. There wasn't much concern over his absence, although Slim wondered out loud, "I wonder where he is?"

No one answered, and they went to bed.

Around three-thirty in the morning, they were all awakened by a loud crash out on the porch and the door slamming.

"What's goin' on here?" questioned Pete as he sat up in bed.

The other hands were awake. When someone turned on the light, they all saw George, stumbling and staggering to his bunk. George fell onto his bunk and passed out. He hadn't even taken off his clothes.

"Just George, comin' in drunk," said Will. "Let's try an' get some more sleep. This night is almost over."

Slim turned off the light and everyone tried to go back to sleep, despite George's snoring.

The next morning, Will, Pete, Kent and Slim rolled up their bedrolls and put them in the back of the truck. George was still sleeping when the men went to breakfast.

"Where's George?" asked Tom, when the men entered the kitchen.

"He's still in his bunk," answered Pete. "He came in pretty late last night."

"I'll get him out!" said Tom, leaving his half-finished breakfast on the table.

He went to the bunkhouse and saw George still sleeping. He went to the barn, got a bucket, went back to the bunkhouse, and filled it with water. He only debated in his mind for a second whether to drip the contents of the bucket a little at a time on George or to let him have it all at once.

I'll let him have it all at once, thought Tom. *That'll probably be the best.*

Tom splashed the contents of the bucket on George all at once.

George quickly sat up, wiping the water from his face. Then he laid back down. Tom went back to the bathroom, filled the bucket again and poured it all on George.

George sat up again and wiping the water from his face, said, "Oh, my achin' head. I got a terrible headache! I need a day off!"

"You had a day off yesterday!" said Tom. "If I'd have known you was goin' out an' gettin' drunk, you wouldn't have had yesterday off! You'd better get up an' get your things together if you're goin' to work here! Breakfast is ready!"

"I don't need any breakfast," muttered George. "Just coffee."

George stumbled from his bed, staggering. "Oh yeah, we're goin' out on the wagon today. I'd forgot."

"I wish you'd forgot to come home," muttered Tom as he went back to the kitchen to finish his meal.

George got up, looked around. He saw that he still had his clothes on and said out loud, "I must have been goin' someplace early this mornin'! I still got my clothes on!" He rolled up his bedroll, staggered and weaved with it and threw it in the truck. Being so hungover, he didn't even change his wet shirt before heading to the kitchen.

"Look at that!" said Pete. "The dead has been resurrected!"

George went straight to the stove and poured himself a cup of coffee.

"Cookie, you'd better take George with you," said Tom. The boys an' I will bring out the horses. You know where to go. I got to make another phone call. You boys saddle your horses, I'll just be a minute."

As the men left to saddle their horses, Slim said to the others, "I don't know why Tom's keepin' him on. He's 'bout worthless."

"Tom probably figures we need another hand," said Will.

"We probably do need another hand, not extra baggage," countered Kent.

Soon Tom showed up, saddled his horse and said, "Will, you come with me. We'll lead an' the others can bring the horses. They know where they're goin', so there shouldn't be any trouble.

Cookie an' George will catch up an' pass us an' they should have camp set up by the time we get there."

They rode into the horse pasture, gathered the horses and started out, with Tom and Will leading. They started out at a brisk trot and Will kept looking back.

"They'll pretty well follow," said Tom. "They know where they're goin'. I think they really look forward to this."

"I'm just makin' sure," said Will. "How come you kept George on?"

"We need what we got an' I ain't got the money to hire another one," replied Tom.

Will let the matter go. He wasn't hired to be a consultant.

The better part of two hours had passed. Will noticed that Tom was looking back more often. But Tom wasn't watching the horses, he was looking for Cookie and George. Presently he saw the dust from the truck and appeared to relax.

When Cookie caught up to Tom and Will, he stopped the truck.

Tom asked, "Everything all right?"

"Yep," answered Cookie, smiling. "We did have to stop while George threw up. He tried to do it while we were movin' but he almost fell out of the truck. He's sleepin' now. I'm afraid he ain't goin' to be much help for a day or two!"

"Yeah," said Tom, gravely. "You go ahead an' set up camp. I don't know how much help he'll be, but the rest of us will show up an' can give you a hand."

The cook drove off and George hadn't even woke up.

"That little stop gave the horses a breather," said Tom. "We better get goin' or it'll be dark before we get to camp."

Tom and Will continued on at the brisk trot they'd started out, with the horse herd following. They went through the corrals and big pasture where most all the cows had calved.

When they got to the gate where they'd turned out the cows, it was all new country to Will.

"There's a few streams goin' through here," said Tom. "More than likely we'll find most of the cattle on them streams. But they'll be well scattered. We'll have a lot of ridin' to get every-thing branded."

"How come you don't brand everything in the corral before you turn them out?" asked Will.

"That question has been asked before," re-plied Tom. "But the feed gets short in that big pasture. The feed's good out here an' there's plenty of it. Besides that, the way we do it is the way my dad used to do it. I kinda like doin' it the ol' way. An' my cows don't mix with the neighbor's. Occasionally, we'll find one of the neighbor's cows with ours, but that don't happen too often. There's too much distance involved."

"But you don't feed durin' the winter," said Will.

"No need to," replied Tom. "There's a lot of feed available out here. When we get farther onto the range, we'll come to a big haystack, almost a mile long where my brother puts hay, just in case we have a really bad winter. He's been doin' that for years an' the far end of the stack is black, useless, spoiled hay. I need to tell him to start another stack, well away from the one that's there so we can burn the old hay. We've been partners in this operation ever since Dad died."

THREE
All the Comforts of Home

It was late in the afternoon when they reached the camp. The cook had set up his cook tent, put the groceries and his equipment and bedroll in it. He hadn't started to put up the other tent, leaving that to George while he fixed supper. There was an old picnic table close by, and the cook convinced George to help him move it into the cook tent. It was a struggle for George, but the two men got the table inside. He got a bucket of water and cleaned off the table.

The men turned the horses into the horse pasture, but not before Tom caught a horse and put him into a makeshift corral close at hand.

"I'll use him to jingle the horses in, in the morning," said Tom. "He won't get anythin' to eat tonight, but he'll have all day to eat tomorrow. Now, let's go see 'bout our livin' quarters."

They found George by the other tent. George

was walking around trying to look busy, but not really doing anything. His hands were shaking and he appeared unsteady on his feet.

"Pete," said Tom, "take that shovel that Cookie used to clear away the snow right over here for our tent. We'll have it up in a jiffy. You ain't got much done, George. How come?"

"I'm sick," replied George. "I think I got some food poisoning in town or picked up a flu bug."

"Yeah, you're sick all right. Brown bottle flu, the way I figure," said Tom. "Get outta the way so we can put up this tent!"

George moved a distance away, looking for wood, while the men erected the tent. Pete brought the small wood burning stove in and hooked up the stove pipe.

"While you're just standin' around," Tom told George, "you can rustle up some more firewood. We'll need a fire in there to keep from freezin' tonight. Cookie's already got his fire goin' an' it's warmed up in his tent. George, you're in charge of keepin' that fire goin' all night. Don't let it go out!"

George went around, looking for some dry wood to burn. Tom started a fire with what wood was available when the tent was up.

After the men got their bedrolls out of the

truck, the cook called them for supper. Before they went to the cook tent, Will said, "I don't think I'll unroll my bedroll until the ground dries out in here some. It might be okay after supper."

"Good idea," said Pete. "I think I'll follow your shinin' example!"

"Me too!" said Kent.

"And I shall follow suit," chimed in Slim.

"Well," said Tom, "seein' as you're settin' the example, I ain't so old I can't take a little instruction! Keep that fire goin', George. When you get it built up good, come to supper."

"I ain't too hungry," said George. "I'll just skip supper today."

"Suit yourself," said Tom as he and the other men went to the cook tent.

When they went into the tent, it was warm.

"You got it nice an' toasty in here, Cookie," said Pete.

"Yeah," replied the cook. "No thanks to George. He wasn't any help. If it was up to me, I'd run him back to town an' fire him! If it was up to me, I wouldn't even cook for him! But, I got to cook for everybody so he'll eat. But I'd just as soon feed him table scraps, just like a dog."

"You'll get over it, Cookie," said Tom. "Let's eat."

It was relatively quiet at supper without George and the cook carrying on a conversation, although the cook kept muttering about how worthless George was.

The cook did make a suggestion to Tom. "When Teddy gets here, why not let him help with the cattle an' let George day herd the horses?"

"I don't think that'll work," answered Tom. "He'd probably let the horses go back to the ranch. I don't think he's that good a hand."

"Who's Teddy?" asked Kent.

"He's the high school kid I hire to day herd the horses. He'll be out when school's done. He's a good kid an' a pretty fair hand for his age. I'll hire him permanent when he graduates if he wants to work for me."

The next morning, everyone was up early, except George. He was awake, but still lying in his bunk, not making any effort to get up and get dressed.

The fire was out and as Tom made a new fire and the other men got up and dressed, he asked George, "You still sick, George?"

"I'm afraid so, boss," answered George meekly.

"Well, you stay in camp today an' gather up

firewood for the cook an' our tent. That'll be pretty easy work. I want to see a big pile of wood by the cook tent an' our tent when we get back. We'll be back early in the afternoon."

The men went to the cook tent and Cookie noticed that George was missing.

"Where's George?" he asked.

"He says he's still sick," said Tom. "I'm goin' to leave him here today. He's supposed to gather up firewood. Don't let him sit in here an' drink coffee all day! I see what everyone said 'bout George's snorin'. It was tough sleepin' last night. I'll go out an' jingle the horses in."

The men drank coffee until they heard Tom yelling at the horses. They went out and got their halters. Slim closed the gate after the horses were corralled. They each caught the horses they were going to use for the day. Tom unsaddled his horse, turned him in with the others, and caught a fresh one for the day's work and saddled him. They turned the horses out into the horse pasture.

Then the men rode out to gather cattle.

After George heard them leave, he got up, put some more wood on the fire, got dressed and went to the cook tent.

"Got any coffee left Cookie?"

"There's 'bout a cup an' a half still left," replied the cook.

"I better finish it," said George. "I'd really hate to see your good coffee go to waste!"

"You can finish it, but don't plan on sittin' in here all day. I know Tom gave you some chores to do, so you'd best be gettin' on 'em. I got too much to do today to babysit you!"

George looked a little surprised. "But I'm a sick man!"

"I'll bet you'll be all right when you get all that booze out of your system! I know what you're sick with!"

George didn't say anything, but sat quietly drinking the rest of the coffee. It was beginning to dawn on him that he wasn't the most popular man on this outfit.

He finished his coffee and went outside. "Tom didn't even leave me a horse!"

There were some aspen trees up a small draw and George thought, *There's probably plenty of firewood up there by those aspen, but how can I get it back? I wonder if Cookie will let me use the truck an' drag some back here. I'll ask him.*

George went to the cook tent and when he entered, the cook was doing the breakfast dishes.

"What do you want?" asked the cook. "The coffee's all gone."

"I wonder if I can use the truck to drag some firewood down from those aspen trees up the draw."

Cookie thought a long while and many thoughts crossed through his mind, the first being, *I wonder if he's plannin' on goin' back to the ranch an' quittin' this outfit? That wouldn't bother me none, one less to cook for.*

His second thought was, *Maybe he's actually goin' to gather up some firewood. I'll give him the keys an' see if he gets his bedroll an' saddle an' lights out.*

After the cook weighed his options, he said, as he handed George the keys, "Sure. Here's the keys."

George went to where his saddle was on the corral fence and the cook thought he was leaving. Cookie started toward the truck, but stopped when he saw George get his rope from his saddle and drive away.

The cook stood in the open flap of the tent and watched George drive off. He didn't get his bedroll out of the other tent and his saddle was still sitting on the makeshift corral. Satisfied that George wasn't leaving, the cook went back to his morning chores.

George wound his way through the sagebrush toward the aspen grove. It was rough going, there wasn't a road.

When he got to the aspen, he found a fallen tree, so he looped his lariat around the trunk, half-hitched the rope to the bumper on the truck and drove back to camp.

The cook had finished his morning chores and was making himself a cup of coffee when he heard George drive up. He went to the flap, opened it and saw George dragging the dead tree toward the cook tent.

"Where do you want your firewood?"

"Anywheres out of the way," answered the cook.

George drove behind the cook tent and took his rope off the tree and the truck.

"I'll get another fallen tree an' be right back," said George as he got back in the truck.

He made another trip to the aspen and found another fallen tree. He dragged it back to camp and left it close to the first one he'd brought back.

When he'd made four trips, he started dragging firewood for the sleeping tent. When he'd made four more round trips, he made one more trip. He'd noticed an old mining camp farther up the draw, past the aspen. He decided he'd do some exploring.

He drove up to the mine and immediately noticed an old outhouse. It appeared to be in good condition, better than the old buildings that were in various states of disrepair.

I bet, he thought, *we could use that back at camp. It would be mighty handy!*

George backed the truck up to the outhouse and with some effort tipped it over onto the bed of the truck. He then pushed it farther onto the truck and drove back to camp.

The cook heard him again and was surprised when George came into the tent and asked, "Can you come out here an' help me for a minute?"

"What you need?"

"Just a hand for a minute. I got somethin' an' I don't want to bust it," answered George.

The cook followed George out to the truck and saw only a part of the outhouse.

"What's in the truck?"

"A surprise! I bet you'll be happy when you figure out what it is!"

The cook was surprised when he saw the outhouse.

"You wantin' to make this a resort, George?"

"Not really. But I do think we can all enjoy the comforts of home. Where should we put it?"

"Better put it a good distance from both

tents," replied the cook. "Of course, you'll want to dig a hole first. An' a pretty deep hole at that!"

"I'm still feelin' kinda poorly. Do you think one of the other fellers would dig the hole?"

"Probably not. You'd better do it. They'll be in before too long. Start diggin', when it's deep enough, give me a holler."

The cook left, muttering something to himself about "Deep enough to bury you!" George was starting to get on the cook's nerves.

George was apparently feeling better, but not good enough to do any hard work. However, he started digging and even though the ground was hard, he had a hole about a foot and a half deep.

"That's plenty," he said to himself. He and the cook slid the outhouse from the bed of the truck and centered it over the hole. As they were centering it, Tom and the other hands rode up.

"What's goin' on here?" questioned Tom. "You buildin' a condominium?"

Slim, looking over the situation, said, "He can have the bottom floor!"

All the other hands laughed, but the comment went right past George.

"What do you think of my creation?" asked George.

"What is it?" asked Tom, mockingly.

"Why it's an outhouse!" replied George. "Now we can have all the comforts of home."

"That's all right," said Tom, "but did you get any firewood?"

"Sure, boss. There's four dead aspen trees over there by the cook tent an' four more over by our tent!"

"You probably should have started cuttin' them up," replied Tom.

"Ah," said George. "But you'll like this better! Besides, I ain't got a chain saw."

"Maybe," said Tom, as he unsaddled his horse and put him in the corral.

"Supper's 'bout ready," said the cook. "Go to the creek an' wash up."

"You know," said Will to Tom as they walked to the creek to wash up, "you should have your brother stack some hay up here so you can feed your jingle horse at night."

"That's a good idea an' I've thought of it before," said Tom. "But I've been worried that the deer an' elk would get to it before I could use it for the jingle horse."

"Then why not bring up some fresh hay from your mile long stack?" asked Will.

"That's an even better idea," said Tom. "That stack is fenced an' the wildlife can't get to it. I'll have George do it tomorrow. We'll need about forty-five bales. That George might make a pretty good camp tender, at that! He wasn't much help calvin' the cows. Just a 'go-fur.'"

At supper, the cook asked, "How many calves did you get branded today?"

"We only got twelve," replied Tom.

"Who did the ropin'?"

"Slim. He's a pretty fair roper," answered Tom. "He only missed three throws."

"I'd have done better, but I'm kinda out of practice. An' I caught one calf by one hind leg," said Slim. "I ain't roped anything since last summer."

"You'll have plenty of practice this spring, an' everybody will have a chance to practice up on their ropin'," said Tom.

The next morning, Tom asked George, "You feelin' any better today?"

"Some," answered George.

"Well, I got another little job for you."

"What is it?" asked George, somewhat apprehensive.

"Down the old road, three maybe four miles, there's an old haystack. Take the truck an' go down there an' bring back about thirty bales of hay. Make sure you get the newest hay, on the east end of the stack. Leave the old black hay, it ain't no good. Stack it close to the old corral."

After Tom and the other hands left, George had another cup of coffee, got in the truck and drove down the old road to the fenced-off haystack. He loaded thirty bales from the newest end of the stack, then took a little break. He fell asleep.

He woke up about an hour later, looked at his watch and decided he better get back to camp. He drove out of the stackyard, not closing the wire gate behind him.

Driving back he hit a rock and some bales fell off. He saw it, but kept going. When he got back to camp, he was surprised to see Tom and the other hands already there. Without saying anything, he drove close to the corral and started unloading the hay.

When he had the hay unloaded, he went to the cook tent to eat. He found the other hands just finishing their supper. Apparently, he'd slept longer than he thought.

"Did you all leave anythin' for me?"

"Yeah," said the cook. "It's still on the stove."

George fixed his supper from the stove as the other hands scraped their metal plates and put them in the wash tub on the stove. When George finished, he put his plate in the wash tub.

"Scrape off your plate before you put it in the cleanin' water," commanded the cook.

George gave the cook a funny look, but said, "Yes sir!" and went to the sleeping tent.

When he entered the tent, he found the other hands stretched out on their bedrolls.

"You guys brand many calves today?" asked George.

"We only got nine branded," answered Tom. "We'll be gatherin' more cattle in the future."

"That outhouse you found is a mighty nice addition to our camp," said Kent.

"In acknowledgment of your discovery, I think we should start callin' you 'Outhouse,'" said Pete.

"Yeah," voiced Slim and Kent, laughing.

"Lay off you guys," said Tom. "George, you better be ready to ride tomorrow. We'll be gatherin' more cattle an' brandin' more calves. Your horses ought to be pretty fresh, although I don't think there's any buck in any of them."

FOUR
Branding Time

The next morning after breakfast, Tom rode out and brought in the horses. Each man went into the corral and caught the horse he was going to ride for the day. Each man except George.

George got his rope off his saddle and entered the corral swinging a loop. He threw the rope and it settled over a horse's neck.

Before Tom could say anything, George had the horses milling and running around the corral. One horse ran into Will, knocking him to the ground. Will got up, slowly.

"Put your rope down!" yelled Tom. "You don't need to rope any of these horses! You all right, Will?"

"I think so," replied Will, stretching to see if he was. "A little stiff, maybe."

"From now on, George," said Tom, "I'll catch your horse for you! You stay out of the corral!

You'll get everybody banged up tryin' to catch your horse. An' you ain't even caught one of your horses. You caught one of Kent's!"

"I appreciate that," said Kent, "but I think I'll use this one today." Kent was being quite sarcastic, but everyone else smiled at his remark.

"Can you ride today, Will?" asked Tom.

"Sure," answered Will.

The men saddled their horses quietly. George was trying to make conversation, but to no avail.

The men mounted their horses, with Will getting on a little stiffly. Tom rode up beside him and questioned, "You sure you're all right, Will?"

"Yeah. Just a little stiff."

The two men rode off together, with the rest following. George was the last man, trailing, riding alone.

"I never should have hired George," Tom told Will. "He's been nothin' but trouble since he showed up."

"Well," said Will, "live an' learn."

"The employment agency said he had good references," said Tom.

"But, I'll bet you didn't call the references," countered Will.

"No, I just went on what the employment

agency said. Except for George, this would be one of the best crews I've ever had."

"Into each life a little rain must fall," said Will, trying to be philosophical.

"Maybe you're right," said Tom. "But sometimes it's tough to make the best of a bad situation."

They rode on for a few miles at a brisk trot, then Tom stopped the riders and sent each one in a different direction to gather cattle. He told them where they should eventually meet and hope to get there.

"George, you come with me," he said. "We'll take a smaller circle an' be waitin' for everybody when they show up."

Tom and George gathered a few cattle and eventually ended up at a place where the brush had been thinned out.

"We've been usin' this place to brand calves ever since I was a kid," said Tom. "We'll just wait here till the others show up with whatever cattle they find. Gather up some sagebrush an' we'll start a fire an' get the irons hot. We'll be ready when they show up."

"Got any coffee?" asked George.

"Nope," came the curt reply.

Soon, the other riders started coming in,

driving the cattle they'd found ahead of them. Slim was the last to show up, but he brought a fairly large bunch of cattle with him. Tom went out to meet him and asked, "You have any trouble?"

"Not really," said Slim. "A few cows wanted to go off in another direction, but I brought 'em all."

"Good! You roped before, who's turn is it today?"

"I don't know," said Slim.

"Well," said Tom, "everybody will get a chance. We'll split it up that way."

"Fair enough."

With all the hands and the cattle they'd found, they started branding. Will and Kent did the roping, Slim and Pete kept the cattle gathered and George helped Tom on the ground.

It wasn't long before they had all the slick calves branded. They took the irons out of the fire and moved them around in the dirt to cool them off. Tom counted the ear pieces he'd cut off when he earmarked the calves.

"Thirty-two," he said, as he entered the figure in his tally book. "We're makin' progress!"

When the irons had cooled, they mounted their horses and rode back to camp.

The procedure was the same for the next few weeks. One day, upon arriving in camp, they all noticed a different pickup in camp.

"What's that?" questioned George.

"Teddy has arrived," said Tom. "My brother brought him out."

"Teddy? Who's that?" asked George.

"He's our jingle boy," replied Tom. "Now we can turn the horses out durin' the day. Teddy will day herd 'em."

The men went to the sleeping tent, took off their chaps and went to the cook tent. Teddy was in there, visiting with the cook.

Teddy got up and shook Tom's hand. "It's good to see you again," said Tom. "So, school's out. Did you graduate?"

"Yes sir!" replied Teddy. "An' it's good to see you! Graduation don't come till next year."

Tom introduced Teddy to everyone, but didn't make any comments.

Teddy was a high school student, about sixteen. He was a well-mannered youngster and had worked for Tom before.

"I put my bedroll in my usual place in the sleepin' tent," said Teddy. "Do I get the same horses this year?"

"Yep," replied Tom.

Tom then went over and shook hands with his brother and introduced his brother to everyone.

After a little visit, Tom's brother said, "I've got to be gettin' back. Anythin' you want from the ranch?"

"No," said Tom. "Let's see, what's the date today?"

"Today is the twenty-ninth of May," answered Tom's brother. "Memorial Day."

"Okay. We'll gather the yearlin's an' have them at the corrals in ten days. Can you call the truckers an' have 'em parked there?"

"Sure! Ten days, huh?"

"Yep! Ten days."

Tom's brother left and Tom and Teddy visited during supper. George was strangely silent, listening to the conversation.

During the conversation, Tom told Teddy, "You'll be glad to know that George brought up some hay to feed the jingle horse you keep in during the night."

"I appreciate that, George," said Teddy. "But I bet my horse will appreciate it more!"

"You bet, Sonny!" said George.

"That's Teddy," said Teddy adamantly.

"You're gettin' big enough now, maybe we ought to shorten that to 'Ted,'" said Tom.

"Whatever you say, Tom."

The following day, the men caught their horses and helped Ted take the horse herd out of the night pasture. When they got to where Tom wanted to graze the horses, they left Ted and went out to brand calves.

Eight days later, they started gathering yearlings from another area of the range that was fenced off. It took two days to gather the six hundred head or so of yearlings. On the day the trucks were supposed to be at the corrals, they gathered them and started toward the corrals. The trucks were already at the corrals with one backed up to the loading chute.

Tom figured they had all six hundred head and they were circling around in front of the gate to the corrals.

"Don't yell," said Tom. "Just take 'em slow an' easy. They're gettin' closer to the gate each time they go around. Don't get in a rush!"

George was watching the cattle, but couldn't see where they were getting closer to entering the corral. He got impatient. He took his rain slicker off his saddle and, swinging it over his head, spurred his horse toward the gate where the cattle were milling around. His horse was surprised and started bucking toward the cattle. George kept swinging his slicker over his head.

Tom saw what George was trying to do and hollered, "Stop! Don't do that!" But it was too late.

The yearlings, being spooked, started running in all directions. The men couldn't hold them.

By the time George got to the gate, the cattle had all scattered and were gone. George had made it to the gate, but hadn't got a single yearling inside the corral.

Tom was mad and let out a string of cuss words that let George know just what he thought of him and his ancestors. And he repeated himself, more than once.

The crew gathered in front of the corrals where Tom was cussing out George.

"That's as close to a stampede as I ever seen," said Pete. "There wasn't no holdin' 'em. They'll be tougher next time."

"I never seen nothn' like that either," said Kent.

"Me neither," added Will.

"The same for me," said Slim.

"You guys gather what you can an' if you get any, load 'em on the trucks," said Tom. "Get a count on 'em. George, you come with me.

You're done. I'm takin' you back to the ranch. You can get your stuff an' vamoose, pronto! I've had enough of you, your sickness, your snorin', everything 'bout you! Follow me George an' don't say nothin'!"

Tom was still mad and rode off toward camp. George followed. He didn't even tell the other hands goodbye.

It was a quiet ride back to camp and Tom was still fuming mad when they got there. He didn't even go in the cook tent.

"Unsaddle your horse an' leave him in the corral. Put your saddle in the truck an' get your bedroll from the tent. Gather up everything you got. I'll be there just to see that you only get your own stuff!"

The cook heard the commotion and came out from the cook tent. He asked, "What's goin' on out here?"

"George has decided to leave us, with a lot of help from me," said Tom.

"Fired, huh." It was more of a statement rather than a question. Unmindful of George's feelings, he added, "Good riddance!"

"I'll be back later, Cookie. Keep some supper warm for me. Get in the truck George!"

Tom wasn't being too mindful of George's

feelings. He got in the truck, started it and began driving toward the ranch.

George started to say, "I'm really sorry ..." but Tom cut him off.

"Don't say nothin'! I'll give you a check when we get to the ranch an' don't you ever come back!"

The ride to the ranch was rough, but silent. Tom was going too fast for the conditions. But he wanted to get rid of George. At the ranch, Tom parked the truck by George's car, watched while he loaded his bedroll and saddle into the car. He was surprised to see a strange car in front of the house.

When the stuff was loaded into George's car, Tom asked, "You got anythin' in the bunkhouse?"

"Nope," said George.

"Then come to the house. I'll get you a check. Although you ain't worth it."

They went to the house, without saying anything to the lady sitting on the porch. Tom went to his desk, got out a checkbook, looked at the calendar, did some figuring in his mind and wrote a check out to George.

Giving it to George, he said, "Here. Now get

out of here an' don't you ever dare show up here again!"

George took the check, looked at it and left without saying "Thanks."

Tom followed him out to the porch and watched until George got into his car and drove off. He made sure George was a long way down the road before he turned to the lady waiting on his porch.

FIVE
The New Hand

When Tom faced her, she asked politely, "Are you Mister Zimmerman?"

"Yes ma'am," answered Tom.

"First of all, I'm not a 'ma'am.' I'm Michelle Dougherty. Folks just call me Mike."

"What can I do for you, Mike?"

"I'm looking for a job and I heard that you might be looking for some hands," replied Mike. "I've been waiting quite a while and was beginning to think you weren't around."

"My crew is out on the wagon now, but we don't have any room for women. I just let that guy go, he wasn't no good."

"I have my own bedroll and my own tent. I can ride as good as any man and can rope better than most. I know cattle and horses, being raised on a ranch."

Tom was beginning to show some interest.

He'd just fired George and was a man short. "Come inside here an' we'll talk. You can tell me about yourself."

They went inside the house after Tom made sure George was well down the road.

Mike told Tom about her past experiences. She was in her late twenties or early thirties. It was hard for Tom to tell, as suntanned as she was. Tom didn't ask, knowing that a woman doesn't like to reveal her age.

As Tom listened, he became more impressed with regard to Mike's qualifications.

Finally, when Mike had finished, he said, "I guess we could give you a try. I don't know how the other hands will react to havin' a woman in camp. But we'll give you a try. If you work out, you've got a job. If not, I'll bring you back."

"Fair enough," said Mike. "And don't worry about the other hands, I've already heard most all the cuss words. They don't bother me at all."

"I'm not worried about that," said Tom. "They all seem to be pretty decent hands. I've never had a woman in camp before. Put your bedroll, tent an' saddle in the truck, we'll be headin' out right directly."

They talked as Tom drove back to camp. The

more they talked, the better Tom liked Mike. But he was concerned how the other hands would react to a woman in camp.

It was well after supper when they arrived in camp, but still before dark.

"Come in the cook tent an' we'll get somethin' to eat," said Tom.

"I'll set up my tent first, while there's still daylight," said Mike, as she lifted her tent out of the truck. She got her bedroll from the truck then asked, "Can I put my saddle on the fence?"

"Sure," said Tom.

The other hands came out of the cook tent along with the cook. Teddy was with them, having put the horses in the night pasture.

Tom introduced Mike to everyone by saying, "This is Michelle, but she goes by Mike. She was lookin' for a job, so I hired her to replace George."

"She don't need to do much to replace George," said Pete. "I'm glad he's gone! You should have run him off earlier!"

"Never should have hired him in the first place!" said Kent.

"We'll find out what kinda hand Mike is tomorrow. I guess you can tell, Mike, the hand you're replacin' wasn't well thought of here."

Will asked, "Need a hand settin up that tent, Mike?"

"Nope," replied Mike, unrolling the tent. "It'll set itself up right directly."

The hands watched as Mike's tent popped up and open. They were surprised to see that she could walk inside the tent upright. She put her bedroll inside the tent, then put her saddle on the corral fence. It had only taken her about ten minutes. Tom was impressed.

"Where do I wash up?" she asked.

"Down at the creek," said Tom. "I'll go with you. I need to wash up, too."

The men watched the two go to the creek without saying anything. Slim looked over Mike's saddle.

"That's a pretty good outfit she's ridin'," he said.

"Yeah," said Pete. "But I didn't see no bridle hangin' on it."

When Mike and Tom returned, they went right to the cook tent. Before entering, Tom asked Will, "How many yearlings did you gather after I left?"

"I counted four hundred sixty-seven onto the truck," said Will.

"Good! That's better than I thought you'd do.

Let's see," said Tom, pulling out his tally book and pencil. "Four sixty-seven from six hundred makes a hundred thirty-three still left. You guys did a whole lot better than I thought. Are the trucks still there?"

"No," said Will. "They said they'd be back tomorrow afternoon."

"Good! Cookie, this here's Mike. I hired her to take George's place," said Tom.

Casting a somewhat disapproving look toward Mike, he said, "Well, she can't be much worse than him."

"We'll give her a try for a couple of days an' see how it goes," said Tom.

"Sit down an' fill up your plates. There's plenty an' it's still warm," said Cookie.

They ate while the cook asked Mike questions. She answered as politely as she could, between mouthfuls. When they were done eating, Mike said, "That was a delicious meal, Cookie. The sourdough biscuits were tremendous. I wish I could make them that good!"

The cook was impressed. It was rare when he got a compliment other than "that's good" from the hands. Words like tremendous and delicious were seldom heard in his cook tent!

While Tom and Mike were eating, the men

were outside talking about the new hand. Everyone had questions about how good she could be.

Slim said, "I'll bet she's pretty good. She's got a good saddle!"

"But I didn't see no bridles," said Kent.

"But did you see her suntanned face?" asked Will. "I'll bet she's ranch-raised an' has plenty of ridin' time under her belt."

"It's a good thing George got that outhouse," said Pete. "Everyone can have some privacy."

Tom and Mike finished eating and came outside the cook tent. Everyone had questions to ask Mike, but they remained silent, probably thinking it was courteous. They all stood outside the tent as Tom told Mike about their procedures.

When Tom was done, Mike said, "I've had a long day, I think I'll turn in. Goodnight boys."

Everyone said, "Goodnight Mike," except one. Somebody said "Goodnight ma'am."

Mike immediately said, "I'm not a 'ma'am.' I'm Mike!"

She turned and went to her tent.

The men went in their tent, grinning, and before they went to bed Tom said, "Don't none of you boys be botherin' the lady durin' the night. We'll find out what kind of hand she is tomorrow. If she does good, she stays. If not, she goes.

Let's hit the sack. It hasn't taken long for the cattle to scatter. We've got some rough days ahead of us."

The next morning, Mike came out of her tent. She had her chaps on and was carrying a few bridles. One was a snaffle, one was a half-breed and one was a spade bit. She asked, "What should I use on my string?"

Tom sized up her bits and said, "You can use any of them on my horses. They haven't been used in a spade bit, but they were all broke in a snaffle bit. You can use any kind of curb bit on 'em." Tom pointed out the horses she was to use while on the ranch. "You get George's ol' string," said Tom.

Mike memorized them, carefully noting each one's features, then asked, "What was the last one he used?"

"The bally-faced bay," answered Tom.

"Well then, we don't want to use him today, although I really like the looks of him. You pick out the horse that has been used the least and I'll ride him."

With those comments, Tom found a new respect for Mike. He liked people that were considerate of horses. He pointed out a sorrel and said, "Use him today. George hadn't used him for four days. We all just go in the corral easy an' catch the horses we want. George came in one day, a swingin' his lariat rope an' got our hand, Will, knocked over an' almost trampled. All my horses are easy to catch an' there wasn't no need for that. I should have fired him then, but didn't."

Mike took the other two bridles back to her tent, keeping out the snaffle bit.

When she returned, she asked, while she was saddling the sorrel, "Was there anything this feller, George, did right?"

"Well," said Tom, "he did gather up a lot of firewood for our tent an' the cook tent, an' he did find that ol' outhouse an' bring it back. Really, that was the best things he did."

"Then," said Mike, "I've got two things to thank him for!"

The other men had been listening and when Mike said that, Pete asked, "Two things? What are they?"

"The first thing is the outhouse," said Mike. "Not many of them in a cow camp. The second is him getting run off when he did. I wouldn't have a job if he hadn't done that when he did!"

All the men laughed.

Slim asked Mike, "Where did you have your

bridles an' chaps? I didn't see 'em tied on your saddle yesterday."

"They were rolled up in my bedroll," answered Mike. "Those bits are pretty nice and I like to take good care of them."

Tom said as they rode off, "Today might be pretty rough. I imagine only the wildest of the yearlings are left. An' they all got a good scare yesterday. But we need to bring everything an' corral 'em all."

When they got to the yearling pasture, Tom sent the riders off in different directions. "If any of you get to the corrals first, just keep your cattle millin' out in front, by the gate. Don't nobody be pullin' a fool stunt like George."

"That goes without sayin'," said Kent.

The men headed out, knowing there might be some hard riding later that day.

They gathered all the yearlings they could find and everyone pushed them slowly toward the corrals. Nobody got in a rush. As they approached the corrals, they slowed down. The cattle were milling around outside the gate. A few were stopping by the gate, looking in, then continuing to mill around.

Finally, after what seemed like an eternity,

a few yearlings started into the corrals and the rest of the herd followed. When Slim closed and latched the gate behind the last one, Tom let out a big sigh of relief.

"I was afraid we'd just about have 'em an' one of them semi-trucks would show up an' spook 'em."

"One of them big trucks did show up, but the driver saw what we were doin' an' stopped a good ways off. He even turned off his engine," said Will.

"That driver must be a cowman for sure!" exclaimed Tom. "I sure want to give him a big thanks! We can turn our horses in this corral. It ain't bein' used for anything."

All the hands took off their chaps and the bridles off their horses, hung them on the saddles and turned the horses loose. They then went to loading the yearlings. The driver would call out how many he wanted for each section of the trailer and the hands would count that many and push them toward the loading chute.

When they had loaded all the cattle onto the trucks and the last truck was pulling away, Tom said, "That was a good job, fellers, an'… ah, lady. I'm glad it's over. We can take a little time an' rest up some before we start back to camp. I swear, I ain't walked as many miles since last year, when we shipped."

After a brief rest, the hands bridled their horses, mounted and started riding back to camp.

Will and Pete rode back together, and Pete said to Will, "She sure knows how to get on, don't she." It was more of a statement rather than a question.

"Yep. An' I'll bet she's a better hand than we think."

"You're probably right," said Pete.

On the way back, Tom explained to Mike how his cow camp worked. When he got done, Mike said, "That isn't much different than other cow camps I've been in."

"I think," said Tom, "that you'll probably have a chance to rope some calves tomorrow."

"You want to find out what kind of a hand I am, huh?" questioned Mike.

"Well … ah … yes!" replied Tom, stammering and stuttering.

Mike had a way of getting right to the point and in this particular instance, it made Tom a little uncomfortable. He changed the subject as fast as he could and the ride back to camp wasn't as stressful as it could have been on Tom.

While Tom made idle conversation riding back, Mike thought to herself, *The test comes tomorrow. I'd better be ready! It seems to me that cowboys in a cow camp hold a higher standard for women than they do for themselves! I suppose women are a little out of place in a cow camp. I'll do my best to change that!*

After they'd unsaddled their horses at the cow camp, the cook told them, "Supper will be ready in about half an hour. I even baked a cake while you were gone!"

Tom looked surprised. Cake wasn't a common occurrence in a cow camp. "I wonder if Cookie is tryin' to impress Mike. She did compliment him quite highly last night after supper." Tom quit talking to himself when Will and Kent showed up.

"Were you talkin' to us?" asked Will.

"Nope," answered Tom. "Just talkin' to myself."

"Come on now, Tom," said Kent, "you can carry on a more intelligent conversation than that!"

"Well," said Tom, as he walked toward the sleeping tent, "you might be right at that! We can rest up some before supper. Mike, you can come in our tent here an' visit some before supper if you want."

"No thanks, Tom," replied Mike. "I think I'll

see if I can give the cook a hand after I wash up."

Tom was surprised. "I doubt if he'll let you," he said and went inside.

Undeterred, Mike went to the creek, washed and went to the cook tent. She opened the flap of the cook tent, stuck her head inside and asked, "Cookie, can I give you a hand?"

Without being invited, she went into the tent.

The cook heard her and without looking up, said gruffly, "Supper will be ready shortly."

Looking up, the cook saw that it was Mike and tried to apologize for his rough tone of voice. "I'm sorry, ma'am, I did ..."

Mike interrupted him. "I'm not a 'ma'am,' I'm Mike!"

"I am truly sorry, ma ... er, ah, Mike," stammered the cook. "There ain't nothin' you can do here. I got everything under control."

"Perhaps I could set the table for you," said Mike. "Where's the silverware and napkins?"

"They're on the end of the table. We ain't got no napkins, we use paper towels." answered the cook.

Mike got the roll of paper towels, tore off eight separate sheets, folded them in half and placed them on the table. She then got eight sets of silverware—knife, fork and spoon—and placed each set on a napkin. Satisfied that the supper table was properly set, she looked around for something else she could do.

Not finding anything, she asked, "What can I do now?"

"Well, ma … ah, Mike, you can holler at the men that supper will be ready as soon as they wash up."

"I won't holler, I'll go get them," said Mike.

Mike walked to the men's tent and not having a door to knock on, asked loudly, "Are you decent?"

"Sure," said someone. "Come on in!"

Mike opened the flap, stepped inside, quickly glanced around, taking note of the condition inside, and said, "The cook told me to get you. Supper will be ready when you've washed up. Better hurry, or I'll eat it all before you get there!"

She was a bit surprised that the men's living quarters were as clean, neat and organized as they were.

SIX
Evaluation

Mike stepped aside as the men filed out of the tent to wash. She even held the flap open for them, then went directly to the cook tent. She was waiting outside the cook tent when the men arrived and held the flap open for them as they entered.

As they entered the tent, Pete said in a softened voice, "Besides a new hand, it looks like we got a doorman, or, ah, woman, to boot!" He said it while grinning, but the other's that had heard him laughed out loud.

Mike also heard it, and grinning herself, said, "Don't expect this every night!"

Tom was the first one in the tent and let out an exclamation of surprise when he saw the table set as it was. "What's this?"

"The plates are on the end of the table," said

the cook. "Get one, come to the stove, I'll dish you up. You can sit anywheres you want, I didn't have time to make name tags. Biscuits are on the table."

"This is gettin' pretty fancy for a cow camp," said Pete. "But I could get used to it real fast."

"Me too!" exclaimed Kent.

The cook dished out everyone's supper—steak, fried potatoes and canned peas.

Slim was the last of the men in line and when Mike got behind him, he stepped aside and said, "You go ahead of me, Mike."

"No," said Mike. "I was the last one that showed up, so it's proper for me to be the last in line. You go ahead, I insist!"

When everyone had sat down, Pete said, "There's an extra plate! Who's that for?"

"Don't forget Teddy," said Mike.

"Oh yeah, the jingle boy," said Pete. "I forgot about him. He should be comin' in pretty soon."

"He'd better hurry," said Slim. "There might not be any cake left for him!"

"I'll make sure there's cake for him!" said Mike.

"Have you taken a likin' to him?" asked Will.

"Well, yes," answered Mike.

"Lucky boy!" said Pete.

"He reminds me of my little brother," said Mike.

With a woman present at supper, the men had taken off their hats to eat, a courtesy not usually shown in a cow camp. The men were a little uncomfortable. They ate slowly and didn't talk much.

"Can you pass the biscuits, Will?" asked Kent. "That is, can you PLEASE pass the biscuits, Will?" Kent corrected himself with a woman present, blushed some and reached for the plate Will was handing out to him. He took the plate, and said, "Thank you!"

Tom saw and heard the exchange and although the crew was polite enough at supper, the added courtesy didn't go unnoticed. Civility in a cow camp among men was kinda rare, although this crew got along well since George had left.

Mike also noticed this and smiled.

Ted entered the tent and the cook said, getting up from his place, "Your plate's on the end of the table. Get it an' I'll serve you up."

Ted was taken aback a little with the cook's comments. This wasn't the normal routine.

As the cook filled Ted's plate, he whispered, "Take off your hat an' your chaps."

"Huh?" said Ted, not hearing him.

The cook pointed toward his head. Ted looked around and saw that no one else was wearing a hat and took his off. He ran a hand through his hair, trying to straighten out what he could. He hadn't brushed his hair and it stood out in all directions. He took off his chaps and tossed them in an unused part of the tent. He put his hat on his chaps.

Having filled Ted's plate, the cook said, "Your place is at the end of the table, next to Mike."

Ted sat down and Mike asked him, "How was your day, Ted?"

"It was okay. The paint horse keeps tryin' to sneak back, but he did it last year an' I was ready for him. I never let him go back last year an' he won't make it this year."

Mike smiled and thought, *He has the makings of a good hand. Determination is there.*

Ted said, "There's a few horses missin' some shoes."

"Who's?" asked Tom.

"One of yours," replied Ted. "An' one of Will's, two of Pete's an' Slim's an' one of Kent's. All of the horses that George used are missin' at least one."

"Mike, looks like you've got the work cut out

for you," said Tom. "We'll get to it one of these days. This ground ain't so rough that a horse can't go barefoot for a few days."

Mike, looking at Ted, asked, "Did you wash behind your ears?" She noticed that Ted was sunburned except where his hat covered his eyes.

"Nope," answered Ted. "I just splashed some water on my face to get rid of the dust."

The men laughed at Mike's question and Ted's response.

"Don't laugh, gentlemen! I noticed that none of you washed behind your ears either," said Mike, laughing. "Don't worry about it, though, I didn't wash behind my ears either!"

The men laughed again and the tension that had been at the supper table vanished.

"Ted," said the cook, "when you're finished, we have some cake for everyone."

"You don't have to wait for me," said Ted. "Go ahead. Just save me a piece!"

The cook set the cake on the table and cut it into eight pieces.

Tom saw how the cook was making a big production of this and thought, *I better talk to Cookie an' tell him not to go to so much trouble every meal!*

When the men were done, they sat back and

relaxed a little to let their supper settle. Ted had already started on his cake.

Someone said, "Cookie, you sure outdid yourself today!"

"Yes!" replied everyone else, almost in unison.

The men got up, scraped their plates into a garbage bucket, got their hats and filed out of the tent.

"Cookie," said Mike, "that was a marvelous supper! Do you need any help with the dishes?"

"No, ma … ah, Mike. I can handle it. You've done everythin' you could today. You go relax. Your day is over."

"I think I'll go watch the sun go down," said Mike. "Tomorrow afternoon will be a good time to start shoein' my string. I'm too full to start tonight."

"Yes," said the cook, "You go do that!"

Mike left the tent ahead of Tom.

Before Tom left, he said to the cook, "I don't reckin we can expect a meal like that every night. What's the special occasion, Cookie?"

"Well, we've never had a woman in camp. This was her first real supper an' I just thought it might be kinda nice to do things up right."

"You really did great! Like Mike said, 'That

was a marvelous supper.' I just hope the men don't expect it every night," said Tom.

"They can expect it, but I seriously doubt they'll get it," said the cook."

Tom went out to where Mike was standing by the corral. Ted's horse that he was going to use the next morning to run in the saddle horses was standing inside the corral. Mike was scratching him between his ears.

"Mind if I join you?" asked Tom.

"Why, no. Please do!"

"This is the best part of the day," said Tom.

"Could be sunrise is better," said Mike.

"I never have time to admire it in the mornin'," said Tom. "I'm always too busy, what with chores an' the like."

"You should take time. It only takes a few seconds."

"Perhaps you're right," replied Tom. "Are you goin' to be ready to rope tomorrow?"

"Ready as I'll ever be," replied Mike.

"You know the boys will be watchin' you pretty close. I think they're all tryin' to figure out what kind of a hand you are."

"That doesn't bother me," said Mike. "I've been scrutinized pretty close in the past."

"It won't make you nervous, will it?"

"No," said Mike, grinning. "But I might have to miss one on purpose just to prove to the men that I'm human!"

Tom was grinning when he said, "Are you settin' yourself up with an excuse?"

"I might be. I just might be!" replied Mike.

"Well, you just do your best. That George, the guy you replaced, he couldn't hardly rope at all! He missed more than half his throws. But he did get a lot of practice coilin' his rope."

"I expect I'll do all right," said Mike.

"Good," said Tom. "Guess I'll turn in. I hope we have a good day tomorrow. Good night, Mike."

"Before you go, I have to shoe some of my horses according to Ted. Can I do it tomorrow when we're done?"

"Sure," said Tom. "The shoein' equipment is in the back of the truck. I'll give you a hand."

"Thanks," said Mike. "But I won't need it. Good night Tom. I'm going to turn in shortly myself. We will have a good day tomorrow!"

Mike continued to scratch between the horse's ears as Tom left. As the sun went down, she left the horse and went to her tent to go to bed.

The next morning, Mike was up before anyone else, except perhaps the cook. She realized he was up when she heard pots and pans rattling in the cook tent.

Presently, Ted came out of the sleeping tent and went to the corral to saddle his horse.

"Are you up already, Ted?" asked Mike.

"You bet!" replied the youngster. "Tom gets me out early to bring in the horses."

"That makes for a pretty long day, doesn't it?"

"No longer than everyone else's," said Ted.

Making sure the cinch was tight, Ted led his horse out of the corral, mounted and rode off to gather the saddle horses.

Mike watched him go, then walked to the cook tent. "Can I come in Cookie?"

"Sure … er, ah … Mike. Coffee's 'bout ready. Come on in."

"Good morning," said Mike as she entered the tent. "Anything I can do to help?"

"Nope. This is pretty easy, ma … er, ah, Mike. You'll have to forgive me, I can't get used to callin' a woman by a man's name. Help yourself to the coffee."

"I imagine that's quite an adjustment. That's okay, I understand," said Mike, as she poured a cup of coffee.

The men filed in as Mike sipped her coffee and they went to the stove where the cook dished up their plates with hash brown potatoes, bacon and eggs.

Tom was the last to enter. He noticed that Mike hadn't started eating yet and said, "You ain't havin' breakfast this mornin, Mike?"

"Oh yes," replied Mike. "I was just waiting for you."

"Don't be waitin' on me!" said Tom. "Around here, it's first come, first served."

"Yes sir!" said Mike, getting up and getting a plate.

Tom also noticed that Mike wasn't wearing any makeup, except for some lipstick. "You only wear lipstick, Mike? No makeup?"

"I don't wear makeup in a cow camp. Do you think I need it?"

"No! Ah … certainly not," stammered Tom. "But why the lipstick?"

"I just use it to keep my lips from getting chapped," answered Mike, laughing. She saw she had Tom a little flustered and was enjoying it.

"Oh," said Tom, obviously uncomfortable in front of the other men.

"I've got plenty. Do you want some?" Mike's comment got a big round of laughter from the other men.

"Try some, Tom," said Kent. "You might look pretty good in it!"

"Ah, eat your breakfast, boys. Mike, when I want some lipstick, I'll ask for it!"

Another round of laughter from the men and Tom saw that he was the butt of a fairly funny joke. He joined in on the laughter.

After breakfast, they went to the corral where Ted had corralled the saddle horses. Ted ate his breakfast while the men saddled up.

"We're not going to give Teddy a hand turning out the horses?" asked Mike as they trotted off. It was plain Mike was considerate and caring of everyone.

"Nope," said Tom. "He's a pretty capable youngster."

They rode out a few miles and Tom stopped. He sent a few riders off to gather cattle, giving instructions on where to meet, rode on for another mile or so with the rest before he sent them off. It was only him and Mike left and they gathered what cattle they could and waited for everyone else at the meeting place.

While they waited, Tom told Mike, "I generally take the short circle so I can be waitin' at the meetin' place for everyone. The men are all new this year an' don't know the country. If anyone gets lost, I'll have a pretty good idea on where to look for 'em."

"Anyone ever get lost?" asked Mike.

"Not really. One year, I thought someone had got lost, but he'd gathered a big bunch of cattle an' was havin' a tough time bringin' 'em all in. He finally showed up but was a little later than I expected him.

"Another year a feller fell off his horse an' broke his arm. His horse came back alone. We found him an' I had to take him to town to the doc's. I was gone all night an' most of the next day. The other hands used the day to shoe horses. Can you shoe a horse?"

"Yes," replied Mike, "but I'm not as good as a lot of guys are. However, the shoes I put on stay on."

"Good," said Tom. "Each hand is expected to keep his, er … that is their horses shod."

Mike laughed. "Yes, I understand."

Tom had sent the riders out in different directions, giving them all directions on where to meet with the cattle they'd gathered. A few hours later, they'd all gathered and got ready to brand. Tom had hobbled his horse and started a fire. The irons were hot.

"Mike, you an' Will rope, Kent you help me

on the ground, an' Pete an' Slim can day herd," said Tom. "There's probably only 'bout twenty-five calves to brand. We shouldn't be too long today."

Kent hobbled his horse. Will and Mike took down their ropes and moved into the herd after Pete and Slim took up positions where they could keep the herd under control.

Will was the first to catch a calf and drag him to the fire. Kent rolled the calf over on his right side and kept his right knee on the calf's neck while he held the calf's left front leg bent back toward the calf's body. With both hind legs being held by Will's rope and Kent being in the position he was, the calf couldn't get away. Tom branded the calf, earmarked, castrated and vaccinated him.

Mike had been watching and when the calf was branded, she caught a calf and dragged it to the fire. Tom and Kent repeated the same procedure on the calf that Mike had caught.

The morning went well and neither Will nor Mike had missed a throw. When Mike dragged another calf to the fire, Tom said, "You two are keepin' this ground crew pretty busy. Neither one of you has missed a throw yet!"

Will had just turned his calf loose and was

heading back into the herd when he asked, grinning, almost laughing, "Do you want to take a little break? Maybe you need a little time to put on some lipstick!"

Will's comment brought a big laugh from Kent and Mike. Tom also laughed, but not as hard as Kent and Mike.

"No, I don't need a break for anythin'!" said Tom, trying to act angry while he was laughing.

"I do have plenty," said Mike.

Slim and Pete saw and heard the laughter and Pete hollered, "What's goin' on over there?"

Will rode toward Pete while coiling his rope and making another loop, and told him, "I just asked Tom if he wanted to take a little time to put on some lipstick. Mike said she had plenty."

"What did Tom say?"

"He declined," answered Will.

Mike and Will continued to rope calves and drag them to the fire. Mike knew she was being watched, closely, and even thought, *Maybe I ought to miss one, just to show the men I'm human! No, I'll just keep roping. Will hasn't missed one yet. I'll show these guys that I'm really a good hand. Just as good as any of them.*

She almost missed one, she'd caught the calf by one hind leg.

"Sorry, Tom," she said as Kent held the calf down and Kent put the free hind leg into the loop. "There wasn't any way that rope would come free by itself."

"That's all right, Mike," said Tom. "We're all entitled to one mistake."

"But Will hasn't missed one yet!" said Mike.

"Look again," said Kent. "He's coilin' his rope. He's made his first miss of the day."

Will was recoiling his rope. Mike hadn't seen it, but it was a sure sign Will had missed his throw.

"Don't worry about it," said Tom. "Everyone's entitled to a few misses. You haven't missed one yet have you Mike?"

"No," said Mike. "I don't dare miss. Everyone's watching me."

"Don't let that worry you, Mike. All the new hands get watched pretty close," said Tom.

"Maybe I ought to miss one on purpose, just to show these guys I'm human," said Mike, grinning at Tom.

"You don't have to prove that. Just keep ropin'."

They kept branding calves. Finally, Will came back empty-handed and told Tom, "We've got 'em all."

"Good," said Tom, taking the irons out of the

fire. He yelled at Pete and Slim, "Turn 'em loose, boys! We're done for today!"

Kent moved the irons around in the dirt, trying to cool them off, while Tom counted ears.

"Thirty-five today," said Tom. "That's pretty good. I wonder who caught the most calves."

"I think Mike caught the most," said Will. "I missed one an' I don't think she missed any."

"That don't matter. Mike's a good roper an' we're done a little early today. A couple more days of brandin' an' we'll gather the bulls an' scatter them. 'Bout three more weeks of brandin' an' we'll be done."

The next day, they all woke up to a heavy rainstorm. The men ran to the cook tent from the sleeping tent. Their rain slickers were tied on their saddles.

During breakfast, Tom said, "We won't go out today. The calves will be too wet to brand. When Ted gets in with the horses, we'll shoe those horses that need it. I don't have an anvil out here, but there's an old piece of railroad track we can use for an anvil. Shoes, nails, rasps, an' nippers are in the back of the truck. There's also a set of alligators for crimping the nails. A couple of hammers are in there, too. We'll sit a spell an' see if this rain lets up. Got more coffee, Cookie?"

"Comin' right up," said the cook, grabbing the pot and filling everyone's cup.

Ted came in. "The horses are here," he said as he took off his rain slicker.

"Get your breakfast," said Tom. "We won't go out today. We'll shoe horses. You'll get a day off, with pay!"

"I've got to put a shoe or two on my horses," said Ted. "I won't get a day off! But I'll take the pay!"

Everyone laughed and drank their coffee.

SEVEN
Shoeing Horses

When the rain had let up a little, Tom said, "Let's go! Looks like it's clearin' up some."

Everyone filed out of the cook tent and went directly to their saddles, got their rain slickers and put them on.

Pete got the railroad track from the truck and set it on the ground close to the corral, but far enough away to be out of the way.

"Wish we had a stump or somethin' to set this on," he said. "We'll have to get down on our knees to shape our shoes."

"It won't hurt you to get on your knees a little more often," said Slim.

"Huh! You might be right!" retorted Pete.

The men entered the corral to catch the horses that needed shoes. Ted told them what horses were missing shoes and they caught them, took them outside the corral and tied them up.

When Mike entered the corral, Ted said, "Your good lookin' bay horse is missin' shoes."

Mike caught the bay, tied him to the fence and got a pair of nippers to start trimming the horse's feet.

Will walked by and asked, "Need a hand, Mike?"

"No, thank you. I can handle this." She picked up the left front foot and started cutting away the part of the hoof that was overgrown. When she'd cut away all that needed to be cut away, she put the foot down, and went to the left rear foot. Seeing that the shoe was still on, but wearing thin, she pulled the shoe and started trimming the hoof. She repeated the procedure on the right hooves.

When she'd completed the nipping, she went to the truck, found a rasp wrapped in a gunny sack and went back to trimming the horse's feet. When she had all the feet level, she went to the truck, got out four number one shoes and set them by the horse. She took one shoe, placed it on the right front foot to see how much shaping it needed and went to the railroad track to shape it.

Slim came to the makeshift anvil to shape a shoe for the horse he was shoeing and said, "I can shape that shoe for you."

"I've got it," replied Mike, holding the shoe up to make sure it was level. She placed it back on the anvil, pounded on it a few times and satisfied it was level, returned to the horse.

Picking up the left front foot, she placed the shoe on the foot to see how well it fit. It was a good match and she went to the truck, got eight nails and a hammer, and returned to the horse. She held the nails between her teeth, took one and holding the shoe in place with one hand, started to nail the shoe on. When she'd nailed all eight nails in and after cutting off the protruding ends of the nails, she took a rasp, filed a little notch under each nail, took the alligators and crimped each nail over. She then trimmed a little of the hoof with a rasp to make it fit the shoe better. It looked better also.

When she finished the right front foot, she went to the right rear. She repeated the same procedure on the remaining feet. It took her about two hours and she had done a good job. She had worked up a little sweat and it was forming on her forehead, even though it was still raining slightly and a little cool.

Tom and the men gathered around when she was done and complimented her on her shoeing job.

Mike took off her hat and wiped the sweat from her forehead. "I could have done a better job if we'd have had an anvil," she said. "I'm not used to shaping a shoe on a piece of railroad track."

"You did all right!" said Tom. "You don't even have to lead the horse through the mud to see if they stay on, or hide your work!"

The men laughed. Some even hoped they could do as good a job on their horses.

"The horse was easy to shoe. He didn't fight or lean on me," said Mike. "If they're all that good to shoe, I could do four in a day."

Mike asked, "Where's Ted? He knows what horses I ride that needs shoes."

"I'm afraid," said Tom, "that all your horses need shoes. George sorta neglected that."

"You take a little break," said Will. "I'll turn this guy an' catch up your sorrel for you."

"Thanks Will. But I can do that, you've got your own horses to shoe."

"My horses were all fresh shod before we came out on the wagon," replied Will. "It's no trouble."

Mike reshod the four horses she'd been given to ride that day. It took her all day, but when she was done, she said, "I'm glad that's done. I won't have to worry about it."

She didn't just do a partial job, she put four shoes on all four horses. The men did give her a hand, trimming feet and shaping shoes for her after they'd finished putting shoes on their horses. That wasn't done particularly for Mike, they trimmed and shaped shoes for each other.

When she got done, she climbed up on the fence to rest. The men joined her.

She said, wiping the sweat from her forehead, "I feel like I've done a day's work! I'd lay down on the grass and take a little nap if it weren't so wet. Sleep will come easy tonight, and early!"

"It won't be long before supper's ready," said Tom. "You can go to your tent an' lay down, if you want. The boys an' I will go to our tent. We'll call you when Cookie calls us. Let's turn these horses out into the night pasture, boys. Be sure to keep a horse in for Teddy to use in the mornin', he's splittin' some wood for the cook."

Kent caught one of Ted's horses, held onto him while Slim opened the gate and turned the horses out. When the horses had all left the corral, Kent turned Ted's horse loose in the corral. Pete threw him some hay. They were done for the day.

At supper, Tom told the hands, "Come rain or shine, tomorrow we'll get the bulls an' turn 'em out with the cows. It'll be quite a long ride to the bull pasture and a long ride back. As a matter of fact, it'll be a long day."

Tom laughed at his own humor, poor as it was. "We'll need to start earlier than usual. I'll get you up. Better hit the sack early."

The next morning, Tom was up two hours earlier than usual. He got Ted up, walked to the cook tent and got the cook up. On the way, he passed Mike's tent and yelled, "You up, Mike?"

"I'm awake, but I'm not up yet," answered Mike. "I'll be out in a minute."

Soon all the hands were in the cook tent, eating breakfast.

Tom asked, "Are you all ready for a long day?"

"Ready as I'll ever be," said Pete. The rest of the men nodded their heads in agreement.

Mike said, "It's a little cooler this morning. I think I'll take a jacket along."

"Good idea," agreed Tom. "It is a little cooler. Don't forget to put your rain slickers on your saddles. You might need 'em today."

Ted came in for his breakfast. "Your horses are all here," he said as he got his breakfast. "It's kinda chilly this mornin'. Wish I'd have taken a jacket!"

"You can take the horses out after daybreak," said Tom. "Meanwhile, you can get warm in the cook tent, if Cookie will let you."

"He can stay in here, if he wants to," said the cook. Then he added, smiling, "I might have him help with the dishes."

The crew finished their breakfast and went out and saddled their horses.

"Make sure you untrack your horses this mornin'," said Tom. "There's really no buck in any of 'em, but as cold as it is, some of 'em might crow hop a little."

The men followed Tom's instructions and mounted. Mike's horse, the good looking bay she'd shod first yesterday, humped up and jumped sideways when Mike got on. Mike stayed in the saddle and the horse only took one jump. She was soothing the horse, patting him on the neck and talking to him softly. The horses calmed down.

They all headed out at a slow trot. After a mile or so, they stopped, let the horses blow then went at a faster pace. They probably trotted about ten miles, stopping again to let the horses blow.

Upon reaching the bull pasture, Tom sent the riders out in different directions.

"Bring everything," he said. "We'll all meet here, then take the bulls to the cows. It'll probably take 'bout two hours."

The riders rode off in the direction Tom gave each one. Around two hours later everyone, except Will, had showed up. Waiting for Will, Tom said, "Open the gate. We'll let the bulls start headin' toward the summer range. The older bulls know where they're goin'. We'll wait for Will."

Half an hour later, Will showed up. "Sorry I'm late," said Will. "These bulls don't move as fast as the cows, an' there's a few that were fightin'."

"That's all right," said Tom. "I think we got all of 'em. Let's move 'em out. Keep a close eye on 'em. If a few get to fightin', the loser will take out his frustration on anything that's close. Last year, one of 'em upset a rider an' his horse. The rider was on foot an' the bull would have really done him some damage, but another rider got between them an' drew the bull away. There wasn't any harm done, but it was touch an' go for a minute."

They moved the bulls out at a slow pace. Tom rode toward the front, heading the bulls in the direction he wanted them to go. They made progress through the morning, although it was slow.

About noon, they stopped close to a creek and let the bulls drink. They watered their horses.

Pete said, "Wish I'd have grabbed a biscuit or somethin' before we left this mornin'."

"Yeah," said Slim. "I'm gettin' a little hungry myself."

After letting the bulls rest for about an hour, they started them out again. It was slow going. There were a few bull fights and the men didn't try to break them up. The losers were mad and took out their frustration on anything that was handy. A few sagebrush and some oak brush were destroyed.

When they started approaching some cows, they started letting some of the bulls go. About four o'clock they turned the remaining herd loose.

"The bulls will do what they're supposed to do from here," said Tom. "They'll scatter themselves. Let's ride back to camp. It's liable to be dark by the time we get there."

The men headed their horses toward camp. They went at a slower pace, their horses were tired.

When they got back to camp, it was after dark. Ted had already brought the horses in. He'd eaten and was visiting with the cook in the cook tent.

The men unsaddled their horses, went to the creek and washed up and filed into the cook tent.

"Your supper will be ready in about fifteen minutes," said the cook. "Long day, huh," he said. It was more of a statement than a question.

"Yep," said Tom. "I think we're all pretty well bushed. How you holdin' up, Mike?"

"I suppose I'm just as tired as the other guys," replied Mike. "However, supper and a good night's sleep will cure that. I'm looking forward to both."

"Me too!" chimed in Kent.

"Likewise," volunteered Slim.

Supper was eaten in relative silence, everyone being fairly tired. There wasn't any visiting after supper, everyone went to their sleeping quarters and went to bed.

The next morning, they were all up at the regular time. At breakfast, Tom asked, "You all get a good night's sleep last night?"

"I think so," answered Pete. "Although I could use another hour or so."

Tom laughed. "You'll be able to get that tonight. The way I got it figured, we got 'bout two more weeks of brandin', then we're done. Do you have any plans?"

"I'll just have to find another job somewheres," said Will.

"Me too," said Slim.

"I ain't got nothin' else to do but look for a job," said Pete.

"I'm in the same boat, only on dry land," said Kent. He laughed at his own joke.

"What about you, Mike?" asked Tom.

"It's pretty rough to find work, especially riding, this time of year. I think I'll hit up some dude ranches and see what I can find."

As they rode out, Will asked, "You got any ideas on where a feller could find a job, Tom?"

"Some of the ranches up north might need a hand," replied Tom. "Although most of 'em are pretty well filled up. You could check in town at the employment agency. They'll certainly know whose needin' help. You're goin' to try herdin' dudes, huh Mike?"

"I guess so. This time of year it would be pretty rough getting on a cow outfit riding," answered Mike.

"I think that would be the most promising," said Tom.

"Have you done that before?" asked Will.

"No," said Mike. "But I've been told it's easy. Just riding around at a walk, taking care of novice riders. I'm also told that tips are good and a little extra money never hurt anybody."

"I've done a little of that," said Will. "It's pretty borin'. If you get along well with the general public, it can be okay."

The next few days were pretty much routine. Gather cattle, brand, move them farther out on the range. Everyone's roping was good and it was decided that when someone missed two throws, they'd lose their turn and would be replaced by the next hand whose turn it was to rope. It was all done in fun.

One day, when dragging a calf to the fire, Mike asked Tom, "Why don't you do some roping? You've done very little roping while we've been out here. I'd be glad to let you finish my turn."

"You want to see how bad I am?" asked Tom. "Besides that, I'm the only one that can make the earmarks."

Will was helping Tom on the ground and he said, "I can make the earmarks. Why don't you go rope a few?"

"I guess I could do that," said Tom. "Mike,

can you help Will on the ground? Will, make sure you keep the ears in a pile so as I can get a good count."

"Sure," said Mike, "I can help Will. I haven't had a turn on the ground yet, but everyone else has. You can even use my rope and horse."

"I have my own horse an' rope," said Tom. "Besides that, it's a catch rope. It don't miss."

When they'd finished with the calf they were branding, Mike let the calf go, got off her horse, hobbled him and let him go. Tom got on his horse, took down his rope and entered the herd. One throw and he was dragging a calf to the fire.

Tom asked, as he dragged the calf to the fire, "Are you big enough to hold that calf down, Mike?"

"It's not the size that keeps them down, it's the technique," replied Mike. "I can keep them in place."

As Mike held the calf down and Tom kept the rope tight, Will branded, earmarked, vaccinated and castrated the calf.

Satisfied that all was being done properly, Tom said. "Let him up, Mike."

Mike released her hold on the calf and stepped away. As the calf got up, Tom gave the rope some slack and the calf kicked free.

"You know," said Mike, grinning, "we'll be keeping track of how many misses you make."

Mike was kidding Tom and he knew it.

"I'll bet I'm under as much or more scrutiny as you were when you first came," said Tom, smiling. "I pray that I do as well as everyone else."

"You better, or you'll never live it down," replied Mike.

The ribbing was good natured and Tom replied, "It takes a smart man to hire hands that are as good as or better than he is!"

"Wait a minute," said Mike. "We're measuring your abilities, not intelligence!"

"That's probably a good thing!" replied Tom.

Tom roped until they were done. He didn't miss a throw. When they were riding back to camp, Tom told Mike, "I sure do appreciate your givin' me a chance to rope. Thanks. Oh, you ain't tryin' to run this outfit are you? It's just like a woman to try to control everything!"

"I think you know me better than that by now," said Mike, somewhat indignantly.

"I hope you know I'm only kiddin' you," said Tom. "After all, you gave me quite a bit of kiddin' when I started ropin'. I'm just payin' you back!"

"I suppose," said Mike, "in that case, it's all

right. However, I'll be very careful how I tease you in the future!"

Tom's roping proved to be equal to everyone else's and nobody could fault him on his abilities. He roped until everything was branded and never missed a loop.

"That's kinda amazin'," Slim said to Kent as they rode to the fire. "He's roped less than anyone an' he's equal to everyone. He ain't missed a throw!"

"I have a sneakin' suspicion that he's been a top hand all his life," said Kent. "He probably let us do most of the ropin' because he don't need no practice."

"You might be right," said Slim.

The following day, they made another gather. They were supposed to meet at a spot, but when Will and Pete showed up, Tom wasn't there. Mike showed up, pushing a few cows to the little herd.

"Have you seen anythin' of Tom?" asked Will.

"No," replied Mike. "Isn't he here?"

"No, he ain't here," said Pete. "I wonder if he's had some trouble."

There was some speculation as to where Tom was and what might have happened to cause his delay. He was supposed to be the first one to arrive.

Slim showed up and put the cows he'd found with the others. He hadn't seen anything of Tom.

When Kent finally arrived, Tom still hadn't showed up.

"I think we ought to go out and look for him," said Mike. "Something's happened, or he'd be here. I hope he's all right!"

"I think you're right," said Will. "Kent, you an' Slim keep an eye on these cows here. Pete, Mike an' I will go out an' look for Tom."

The three riders left the herd at a fast trot in search of Tom. They each went in a different direction from where they'd come from and different from where Slim and Pete had come from. They needed to cover a lot of ground.

Nobody seemed to take offense at Will's taking charge of the situation. This could be an emergency and there wasn't time to argue over who was the boss. In each's eyes, they were about equal.

Pete topped a small rise and saw a riderless horse grazing in the bottom of a small draw. He let out a loud yell, loud enough for Will and Mike to hear, and rode down toward the horse. He rode right up to the horse, caught him, and started riding up the draw, leading Tom's horse.

Soon, he heard Will's yell from up the draw. He continued up the small draw and presently saw Will, standing on the ground, over Tom.

As he rode up, he saw Tom laying on the ground and asked, "Is he dead?"

"Nope, just unconscious," said Will. "Mike's already riding back to a little stream to get some water. I haven't dared move him, for fear somethin' might be broke. We'll wait for Mike."

Mike showed up with a couple of handkerchiefs that had been soaked in the stream.

"This is the best I could do," she said, getting off her horse and handing the reins to Will.

She went to Tom and applied the wet handkerchiefs to Tom's face, slowly rubbing them.

Soon Tom coughed and started to move. Mike kept the wet rags on Tom's face.

Tom brushed the wet rags from his face and sat up. "What's goin' on here? I've already washed this mornin'!"

"But not behind your ears!" said Mike.

"What happened?" asked Tom.

"You tell us," said Will. "We weren't here to see it."

"The last I remember I was chasin' a wild cow.

My horse fell. That's all I remember. Where's my horse? Is he all right?"

"He's right here," said Pete. "He's okay."

"Good," said Tom. "Now let me up. If you guys … er, folks found any slick calves, they need to be branded." He corrected himself, noting that Mike was present.

"Slim an' Kent are holdin' the cattle a little ways from here," said Will.

Tom got up, staggering a little.

Mike asked, watching him stagger to his feet, "Are you okay?"

"I do have a headache an' my balance is a little off," said Tom. "I must have hit my head on a rock. I'll be all right."

Tom got on his horse, a little awkwardly, not the way he usually swung into the saddle, and said, "I'm ready, let's go!"

As they rode to where Slim and Kent were holding the herd, Tom kept a hold of the saddle horn all the way.

When they reached the herd, Tom said, "Will, you brand. Pete can help you. Kent an' Slim can rope. Mike an' I will do the day herdin'."

Will and Pete hobbled their horses. Will got the irons from Tom's saddle while Pete built a fire. Mike and Tom took up positions where they could best hold the cattle.

Before Mike left, Will told her, "You keep an eye on Tom. I don't think he's a hundred percent."

"Yes," said Mike. "He might have a slight concussion. I'll watch him."

When the irons were hot, Slim and Kent took down their ropes and started roping calves.

In no time they had all the calves branded and Tom rode to the fire. He didn't get off his horse. "I guess we're all done here," he said. "Count the ears, Will, an' tell me what you got."

Will counted the ears and told Tom the total. Tom entered it in his tally book. They took their time riding back to camp, as Tom wasn't feeling up to par.

EIGHT
A Slight Delay

The cook had supper ready when they arrived at camp. They were later than usual. They went to the creek to wash up, but Tom went directly to the sleeping tent.

The hands filed into the cook tent and Cookie noticed one hand was missing. He asked, "Where's Tom?"

"He went directly to his bunk," answered Mike.

"He fell off his horse an' hit his head," said Will. "He was unconscious when we found him. I don't think he's feelin' too good."

"I better check up on him," said the cook. "It's not like him. You can fix your supper, it's on the stove."

The cook went to the sleeping tent and found Tom lying on his bunk. He asked, "You awake, Tom?"

There was no reply from Tom.

Cookie asked again, this time louder and shaking Tom by his shoulders, "Are you awake!"

Again, there was no response from Tom.

The cook went back to the cook tent.

"Tom all right?" asked Slim.

"I don't think so," said the cook. "I can't get him up. I think he's got a concussion an' I've heard you're not supposed to let someone sleep that has a concussion. A couple of you boys give me a hand gettin' him into the truck. I'm goin' to take him to town to the doctor's. I don't think it will hurt to have him checked out."

Everyone got up from the table as the cook took off his apron.

"I'll get the door to the truck," said Mike.

The men went to the tent and a couple of them half carried Tom to the truck. He was awake, but incoherent.

"You want him in the front or in the bed?" asked Pete, jokingly.

"Put him into the front, an' lock the door," said the cook, as he got in on the driver's side. "I don't know when I'll be back, soon as I find out what's goin' on. Just keep on gettin' them calves branded. There's plenty of leftovers available for eatin'. Make sure you do the dishes regular, after every meal!"

Cookie drove off with Tom slouched on the seat of the truck. He was driving pretty fast and Tom was getting bounced around on the seat. The road they were on was little more than a cow path. A time or two, the cook had to reach over and catch him to keep him on the seat.

The cook drove directly to the emergency entrance at the hospital. It was well after dark when he arrived.

"What have you got here?" asked an attendant.

"He fell off his horse," answered the cook. "I don't think anything's broke, but I think he's got a concussion. He's been unconscious, or close to it, ever since we left camp."

"We'll have a look at him," said the attendant. He motioned for another attendant to bring a stretcher. "You can park your truck over there," he said, pointing to the parking lot. "When you get parked, you can come in and fill out the admittance papers."

The cook parked the truck and went in the hospital. He was given a clipboard with some forms on it and told to fill them out.

He looked over the papers. "I don't know the answer to a lot of these questions," he said.

"Fill it out as best as you can. We'll have a doctor look at your friend."

Cookie filled out the paperwork as well as he could and gave it to the nurse behind the admittance desk. "I'll just hang around until you can tell me somethin'," he said.

"Fine," said the nurse. "You can wait over there. The doctor is examining your friend now."

The cook took a seat in the waiting room and promptly fell asleep. It had been a long day for him. He didn't know how long he slept, but was awakened by someone shaking him.

"What's goin' on here!" he exclaimed as he jumped to his feet.

"Hold on there, old timer! I'm Doctor Reynolds."

"Oh," said the cook. "I guess I fell asleep. How's Tom?"

"It looks like he suffered a concussion," said Doctor Reynolds. "We'll need to keep him here for a few days for observation, but he should be all right."

"Well," said the cook, "I'll get a motel room in town an' stay until you say I can take him back to camp. Wait a minute!" he exclaimed. "I can't stay in town! I ain't got no money! My wallet's back at the ranch. I'll have to go back there."

"Tell me the phone number. I can call you when your friend is ready to leave," said the doctor.

"To tell you the truth, I don't know the phone number out there," said the cook. Then he added, laughingly, "I haven't had to call myself for quite a while. But it's in the book, under Tom Zimmerman. I guess I'll go to the ranch an' get some shut-eye. Call me if anythin' develops."

The cook drove back to the ranch. He found everything there in order and went to bed in his own bedroom.

The next morning, he woke up, stood in the shower a good twenty minutes, and dressed in clean clothes. He got his wallet and made sure he had some money. He drove to town and checked with the hospital on Tom's condition.

The doctor told him Tom was conscious, and out of bed walking around, but he wanted to keep him another day for observation.

The cook asked, "Can I see him?"

"Certainly," said the doctor, "if you can find him. He's walking around somewhere."

"He never did like hangin' around, doin' nothin'," said the cook.

Cookie found Tom outside in a small enclosed area.

"How you feelin'," the cook asked as he approached Tom.

"I'm ready to leave here," answered Tom. "But I can't go anywheres. They took my clothes!"

"The doc told me that they want to keep you another day for observation," said the cook.

"That's more than they told me," said Tom. "I wonder how my hands are gettin' along back in camp."

"I wouldn't worry about 'em," said the cook. "They're all top hands. I imagine they'll continue brandin'. I can't see 'em sittin' around camp, doin' nothin'. But if they are, a day off won't hurt 'em. They've earned it."

"I suppose you're right," said Tom. "They're all top hands, the best crew I've had in years. What are you goin' to do today?"

"I didn't have anything planned," replied Cookie. "This was kinda an unexpected trip. I'll just hang around until they turn you loose. What happened, anyway?"

"My horse fell an' I jumped off. I guess I hit my head on a rock or somethin', I don't remember anything after that."

"You don't remember ridin' back to camp?"

"Nope," said Tom.

"You came ridin' in, holdin' on to the saddle

horn with both hands," said the cook. "You un-saddled your horse an' went straight to your bunk. When I came out to check on you, you were passed out. I thought it best to bring you here."

"I guess I appreciate it," said Tom. "But we really ought to be back in camp."

"If you do what the doc tells you, you'll be out of here before you know it," said the cook. "Don't worry about things in camp, they'll be all right."

NINE
A Short Crew

Back in camp, after the cook left with Tom, supper was finished in relative silence, the only comments being expressed were with regard to Tom's welfare. Everyone hoped he would be all right.

"I hope so," said Slim. "He's one of the best guys I've ever worked for."

"Yep," agreed Pete. "I kinda get the feelin' I'm workin' with him rather than for him." There was a general agreement among the hands.

Right before supper was finished, Mike said, "Ted, if you'll give me a hand, we'll do the dishes, then someone else can do them in the morning. Then someone else can do them tomorrow night. I'll try to cook something for supper tomorrow, then, if necessary, someone else can cook supper the next night."

"Good," said Pete. "I'll cook up some bacon in the mornin' an' fix up some pancakes. You all can cook your own eggs to your own likin'."

Without actually taking charge, Mike had lined out the procedure for doing the kitchen chores, although a cook hadn't been delegated.

Ted asked, "What will y'all do tomorrow?"

"I suppose," said Will, "we ought to just continue doin' what we've been doin', gatherin' cattle an' brandin'. Ted, you bring in the horses in the mornin', just like always, an' we'll go to work, just like nothin' happened."

The plan was established, although a certain air of foreboding was present.

The next day, they gathered cattle. When they all met, it wasn't at a spot that Tom would have selected, but it was relatively free from brush.

"Whose turn is it to rope?" asked Will.

"I think it's Mike's," volunteered Kent.

"Okay. I'll brand, Mike can rope. Who can help me on the ground?"

"I'll help you," said Slim.

Without actually saying so, Will had assumed the boss responsibilities, although it wasn't really necessary. They were all good hands and there wasn't a thread of jealousy present. They all realized that they had a job to do and that each could handle anything they needed to do.

When they'd finished branding, Will counted the ears and wrote down the number in his tally book. They put out the fire, cooled the irons and rode back to camp. After they'd unsaddled their horses and turned them loose, Mike said, "Supper will be a little late today. I really don't know what to fix. You boys relax and I'll call you when it's ready."

The men went to their tent to relax.

"I hope she can cook as good as she ropes," said Kent.

"I'll bet she does all right," said Pete. "I'm willin' to bet she does good at anything she tries."

A little longer than an hour later, Mike called the men in.

"Supper's ready! I don't know how it turned out, but I don't think it will make you sick! It's a bunch of leftovers I put together."

"I bet it's great," said Slim.

The men ate, each one complimenting Mike that she'd done a great job cooking.

Mike, noting that the compliments were flowing freely, said, "If you think you can compliment me into cooking tomorrow, you fellers are all wrong! I roped today, so I think whoever ropes tomorrow should do the cooking."

"Fair enough," said Slim. "Whose turn is it to rope?"

"I'm afraid it's my turn," said Kent.

"Good," said Mike. "I'll show you where everything is and you can have at it tomorrow night. Who's going to do dishes tonight?"

"I suppose I could take a turn at it," said Will.

All the camp chores were being divided as equally as possible among the crew.

The following day, the crew went out and branded calves then returned to camp. Kent did the cooking, making the remark, "I really hate doin' my own cookin'. Actually," he continued, "I really don't mind doin' my own cookin', the part I hate is the havin' to eat it!"

The next day was pretty much like the previous two days. The crew went out, gathered cattle and branded. While they were gone, Tom and Cookie returned from town. Tom had been released from the hospital without any restrictions.

The cook was surprised that the hands were all gone when they showed up, but Tom wasn't.

"Where do you think they are?" asked the cook. "Do you think they've all rolled up an' left?"

"No," said Tom. "I imagine they're out brandin' cattle. As good a hands as they all are, they really don't need me!"

"I better start supper. I'll bet they're all starvin'!"

"I'll just hang around until they show up," said Tom. "Maybe you can fix up some coffee."

Tom went to the sleeping tent, saw that everything was in order and went to the cook tent.

"There's some coffee left," said the cook. "I'm heatin' it up now. It'll be ready in a minute. Looks like everythin' is okay here. Even the dishes are done. I'm surprised."

"I'm not," said Tom. "This crew can pretty well take care of themselves."

When the hands arrived back in camp, they all welcomed Tom back. While they unsaddled their horses, Tom asked, "Who's been in charge since I've been gone?"

"Nobody, really," said Slim. "We just sorta divided up the chores an' went from there. We kept on goin', just like you was here. However, at times it did seem like the blind was leadin' the blind."

The crew laughed.

Tom asked, "How many calves did you brand?"

Will got out his tally book and gave the numbers to Tom.

As Tom entered the numbers in his tally book, he said, "Looks like you done all right since I've been gone."

"We done all right," said Will. "How are you doin'?"

"I'm okay. They kept me in for observation. I don't know what for, I wasn't goin' to commit any crimes!"

The crew laughed and they all welcomed him back.

The next day they made another gather. They didn't find many slick calves to brand.

A few more days of branding and they'd be done. They headed out one morning just to make sure they'd branded everything. Tom sent the riders in different directions and they all met at a pre-arranged spot. They did come across some slick calves, and got them branded.

When they returned to camp, Tom said, "I guess tomorrow we can make preparations to head back to the ranch. We're pretty much done here. We'll be spendin' tomorrow night at the ranch. Mike, there's a spare bedroom in the house. You can use it. There's not an extra room in the bunkhouse. Tomorrow, after breakfast, I'll make out your checks. But while you're all here now, I want to say that this is the finest crew I've ever had. I wish I could keep all of you on, but I just don't have the work. If you need a job, my brother can use some help puttin' up hay. Regardless of what you do, you all have a job here next year, startin' around calvin' time. You're all top hands!"

THE END

Other Books by Stu Campbell

Horsing Around a Lot
Horsing Around the Dudes
Humor Around Horses
You Can't Be Serious!
Comedy Around the Corral
More Humor Around Horses
Muddy Waters
Comedy Around Cowboys
The Loner
The Drifter
The Life of a Cowboy
The Wagon
Patience & Persistence

A Young Cowboy's Adventure Series

A Young Cowboy's Adventure
Honey
Surprise!
Intruders
Expectations
Frozen
Advice
Broken
Ginny

Wild Horses for Wild Kids
The Kids Get Horses

About the Author

Stu bases his books on his true-life experiences of ranch life and being a cowboy. He is a graduate of Utah State University with a degree in Animal Husbandry, and has also been a ski instructor, truck driver, and rancher.

About the Cover Artist

Cowboy artist, **R. Loren Schmidt**, is truly a cowboy and an artist. He illustrates from real life experiences from his lifetime of cowboying. A lifetime of dedicated art practice is evident in his expressive and accurate depictions of the contemporary cowboy experience. Loren is most inspired by his friends, horses, and the grand adventures in the backcountry of the West.